Miracle at Del Norte

Robert M. Brunelle

WestBow
PRESS
A DIVISION OF THOMAS NELSON

WestBow Press books may be ordered through booksellers or by contacting:

WestBow Press
A Division of Thomas Nelson
1663 Liberty Drive
Bloomington, IN 47403
www.westbowpress.com
1-(866) 928-1240

Because of the dynamic nature of the Internet, any Web addresses or links contained in this book may have changed since publication and may no longer be valid. The views expressed in this work are solely those of the author and do not necessarily reflect the views of the publisher, and the publisher hereby disclaims any responsibility for them.

Any people depicted in stock imagery provided by Thinkstock are models, and such images are being used for illustrative purposes only.

Certain stock imagery © Thinkstock.

ISBN: 978-1-4497-0879-5 (sc)
ISBN: 978-1-4497-0914-3 (dj)
ISBN: 978-1-4497-0878-8 (e)

Library of Congress Control Number: 2010941176

Printed in the United States of America

WestBow Press rev. date:12/10/2010

Dedication

This book is dedicated to the three people in my life that showed the kindness and the encouragement of Jesus:

To my mother, Martha Brunelle, who inspired me and gave me the confidence to follow the desires of my heart.

To my wife, Terrie Brunelle, who urged and supported me in love to not give up.

To my daughter, Melissa Navarro, who encouraged, edited, and educated me in the art of storytelling.

"I can do all things through Christ which strengtheneth me."
Philippians 4:13

Contents

Preface

This book is a work of fiction. All characters and incidents in this novel are the products of the author's imagination. Any similarities to people living or dead are purely coincidental.

All references to real people, events, establishments, organizations, or locales are intended to provide a sense of authenticity, but are used fictitiously.

Introduction

Rob returned to Robinson's bedside. He poured a glass of water for the inmate. "Here ya go," said Rob as he handed him the glass. Robinson reached out with a shaky right hand and grabbed the glass from Rob. It was then that Rob saw it for the first time. *How could I have missed it?* he thought. *It's the same tattoo.* It was the same green and red serpent on the right forearm of the robber who killed Rob's parents; the robber he had vowed to kill. Rob was stunned and speechless. At first, he could not even think. It was as though his brain was frozen, but slowly it began to thaw, and grew to burn red with hatred for this dying inmate. *Finally,* he thought, *this man will pay for what he did… I'll make sure of it.*

"The steps of a good man are ordered by the Lord, And He delights in his way. Though he fall, he shall not be utterly cast down; For the Lord upholds him with His hand."
PSALM 37:23-24

CHAPTER I

A Desert Storm

A thick, heavy sandstorm was blowing across the desert dunes, blocking out a blue, cloudless sky. On the horizon, a large, shadowy figure plodded across the distant ridge as if in slow motion. Through the flying sand, Corporal Rob Jacobs peered through his binoculars, trying to determine if this advancing form was friend or foe.

The twenty-three-year-old Jacobs had led his five-man reconnaissance squad up the sand dune for a better position to observe the valley below. But the wind and swirling sand made it difficult to stand, let alone see. This sand was not like the sand where they trained on the beaches of Southern California's Camp Pendleton.

They were a close-knit group, having been together even before basic training. It seemed like a lifetime ago, but it was only four years earlier, when a well-tanned Rob Jacobs, carrying his surfboard under one arm, ran through the Huntington Beach sand toward the huge breakers. But today, it was a different type of sand; it was a sticky, dirty, nasty, blowing kind of sand that stung his face. "See anything, Rob?" asked Private Manny Garcia as he adjusted his goggles. "I can't see a thing."

"I think I know why they call it Desert Storm," quipped Rob. "Saw a sandstorm near Las Vegas once. Nothing like this."

"Vegas! Viva Las Vegas!" crooned Manny, doing his best impression of Elvis Presley. "That's where I wish I was right now. Vegas!"

"There's something moving over there," Rob whispered sternly, as he pressed the binoculars tightly up against his eyes. "Oh, it's just a ... lost *camel*," he snickered, momentarily cutting the tension. "Wait, I think I see—"

"What is it, Rob?" interrupted Private Sol Grabel as he dove between Rob and Manny, thrusting his rifle forward toward the valley below. Sol slowly rose to his knees and peered through the blowing sand. "I don't see anything."

The three marines had been high school classmates before joining the corps on the Buddy Plan. They had been varsity football teammates and CIF-State champs. The stocky Sol Grabel played center, the broad-shouldered Manny Garcia, fullback, and fair-haired Rob Jacobs was the quarterback. Rob had turned down a full-ride scholarship at USC, the University of Spoiled Children, as he often called it. Instead, he joined the marines, and now, four years later, he was still calling the plays.

"Get down! Get down! Tank! Tank!" yelled Rob. He and the rest of the squad dove face-first into the sand dune. "Stay down! I don't think they saw us. They might go right past—"

A deafening explosion that shook the ground interrupted Rob's command. The Iraqi tank was firing on their position. Its first round blasted a huge crater right in front of them.

Several kilometers to their right, a fellow marine screamed, "Incoming!"

"Rob! Rob! What the—" yelled Sol as a second explosion sent him, Rob, and Manny tumbling backward down the sand dune. Rob's helmet flew off and rolled a few feet away from him. He reached out, and as he grabbed it, he caught a glimpse at the tattered wedding photo of him and his bride, Jenny, taped to the inside.

A few years earlier, Rob and Jenny were graduating from Huntington Beach High School. They had been together ever since she invited him to the Sadie Hawkins dance. That's when he knew she was the girl he wanted to marry, and he told her so that night. No one was surprised when they got married right out of high school.

Though only nineteen years old when she married Rob, Jenny O'Reily acted much older. The product of dysfunctional, alcoholic parents, she had to grow up fast and learn to take care of herself. She was only twelve when her parents divorced, and she still remembered her father drunk, stumbling through the front door; the many arguments he had with her mother; the emotional and sometimes physical abuse her mother suffered, which led to her mother's own drinking problem. Jenny could have easily fallen in with the wrong crowd and become an addict herself, but thankfully she found support from a local church. There, she became a Christian, finding wholeness in the love of Christ and the fellowship of other believers. She became diligent in reading the Bible, memorizing, and then quoting scripture to fit the situation or occasion. Though skeptical at first, Rob eventually joined her in attending church. In their senior year, Jenny talked Rob into attending a youth rally at the beach. The beach was crowded, with over a thousand teenagers dancing to a live Christian rock band. The music was lively at first but then became more solemn. He had told himself he was just going to the rally because of Jenny, but by the time the youth pastor finished speaking, Rob's heart had softened. When the invitation was given, he bolted to the front of the crowd and accepted Christ as his personal Savior. From then on, it was their faith that cemented and matured their relationship, making their decision to marry young seem less ominous to their peers. Jenny was the best thing that happened to Rob.

Suddenly, another blast from the Iraqi tank cannon exploded, sending the three marines flying and bringing Rob Jacobs back to the reality of war.

"Rob, I'm hit! I'm... hit! I can't... feel my..." gasped Manny as he coughed up some foamy blood that oozed down the side of his cheek. He then stopped breathing, and his eyes appeared to glaze over. Rob reached over and grabbed Manny's arm, but realized it was too late. Private Garcia was dead.

"Rob! Rob!" yelled Sol. "Let's go, sir! Let's go! Manny's dead. We got to go, now!"

Sol helped Rob to his feet and pulled him by the arm down the backside of the sand dune. The Iraqi tank continued to bear down on their position. Rob looked down at his leg and realized he was severely wounded.

"I can't feel my leg," he muttered under his breath. "My leg! My leg! I can't —"

Sol continued to pull Rob's arm as they made their way through the sandstorm. "They say there are no atheists in times like this," Sol whispered to himself. "Lord, help us!"

"I don't think I can make it," Rob declared. "Oh, Lord!"

"Come on, Corporal!" encouraged Sol. "Just hang onto me, Rob. If we can just make it to that old bunker —" The blowing sand partially obscured a burned-out cement bunker that was about twenty yards away. The two struggled toward the bunker as the Iraqi tank fired another round that landed close to their position. Rob's leg was bleeding profusely when they reached the bunker, and the pain was obvious on his face.

"Manny. We can't leave Manny back there," pleaded Rob.

"It's too late. He's dead," replied Sol. "I got to get a tourniquet on that leg of yours." Sol removed the belt from his pants and wrapped it tightly around Rob's leg until the bleeding subsided.

The roar of an F-15 fighter jet grew louder in their ears, punctuated by its missile as it blasted the Iraqi tank into torn, twisted metal.

"We can't leave Manny, Sol. Go get him. Go," pleaded Rob.

"Okay, okay. I'll go get him. Stay put!"

Sol traveled back through the blowing sand to the top of the sand dune. Tears came to his eyes as he looked at Manny's lifeless body. He picked him up, threw him over his shoulder fireman style, carried him back to the bunker, and laid him at Rob's feet.

The immediate threat was over. The tank was destroyed, and other marines were now arriving at the burned-out bunker. A short, muscular, thirty-year-old sergeant with red hair led them.

"I'm Sergeant Edwards," he announced. "You two are lucky to be alive. We called in that air strike just in time, didn't we boys?"

added Edwards as he looked down at Rob. "Corporal, by the looks of that leg, you'll be headin' back home."

"Sarge, is it bad? My leg?" asked Rob. He never heard the sergeant's answer, and woke up a few days later in a hospital bed.

CHAPTER 2

Nightmares

Captain Adam Duval, an army doctor, was making his rounds at the US military hospital in western Germany, where the majority of the wounded were taken for treatment and rehabilitation. Currently, there were twenty-four wounded men there in various stages of recovery. The moans and groans from the more seriously injured could be heard over the squeak of Captain Duval's shoes on the linoleum floor. Drowsy but coherent, Rob waited as the captain read his chart.

"Looks like you might lose this leg, Corporal Jacobs," remarked Captain Duval as he snapped Rob's medical chart closed.

"No, Doc! Don't cut off my leg, please. You can't cut off my leg!" Rob pleaded. "Could ya just give me something for the pain? I can't stand the pain!"

"Corporal, you have already had too much morphine. I can't give you more right now," advised Captain Duval.

Rob was soaked with perspiration. Blood and pus oozed from a twenty-two-inch-long gaping wound. His leg throbbed with pain, and he had to bite his lip to keep from screaming. "Please. Please! Can't you give me something?"

Doctor Duval searched Rob's eyes. "Rrrr," he murmured with pinched brows. "Nurse, give him another 10cc, and let's get him prepped for surgery, stat!" ordered the captain as he stared at Rob. "We'll try to save that leg, son, but no guarantees."

Rob woke several hours later in a hospital room shared by an 18-year-old fellow marine who had lost an arm in a firefight with Saddam Hussein's elite Republican Guard. Still groggy from the anesthetic, Rob tried to focus on his surroundings. He stared at the young, blond occupant of the bed next to him trying to see if he recognized the young marine.

"Finally awake, huh? I'm Private Donny Weeks from Cookeville, Tennessee."

Rob strained to lift his head from the pillow. His body was still under the affects of the anesthetic. He could not feel anything from the waist down, and could not determine if he still had two legs due to the sheet that covered his body.

"Can you see my feet?" moaned Rob. "Do I still have two?"

"Yeah, you're lucky, man. You got two of everything," replied Donny holding up a stump of a right arm, "but we're both goin' home."

"Sorry, man, about your arm," apologized Rob as he glanced over at Donny who forced a smile, then turned and sat on the edge of his bed facing Rob.

"No problem… uh?" Donny said looking inquiringly at Rob.

"Rob. Jacobs. Corporal Rob Jacobs."

"I'd shake your hand, Corporal, but…" quipped Donny, again holding up his stump and forcing a laugh.

Captain Duval, wearing a long white coat, grinned as he entered the room reading a clipboard. Without looking up he asked, "How are we doing, gentlemen?"

"We're just ducky, doc. When do I get to go home?" asked Donny.

"Soon," he replied as he turned to Rob. "And, how are you feeling Corporal?" asked the doctor as he pulled down the sheet and began to examine the bandage on Rob's leg.

As the doctor poked and prodded the cobwebs cleared from Rob's head and the pain began to swell in his leg. "Can you give me something for the pain?" groaned Rob. "I think the anesthetic has worn off."

"You'll be dealing with pain for quite some time. We had to put in a rod that runs from your knee to your foot, metal plates on each side of your ankle, all held together with screws," stated Captain Duval.

"Now you know what it feels like to be screwed, Corporal," chided Donny. "And good luck getting through the metal detector."

Nurse Irene Durham, who entered the room right after the doctor, stifled a giggle at Donny's attempt at humor, but Captain Duval and Rob remained stoic and were not amused.

"Look Corporal, your surgery was successful, insofar as you still have a leg, but you're going to need a lot of physical therapy to even get you upright again," said Captain Duval. "But first things first, we need to make sure you have complete circulation in that leg and that the wound heals properly."

"When will the pain go away, doc?" asked Rob.

"In time, son," replied Captain Duval as he patted Rob's good leg.

Rob watched the doctor walk away, but the affects of the morphine made him drowsy and he struggled to keep his eyes open. The battle ended and his eyelids finally closed. Captains Duval's footsteps echoed down the hallway and faded to silence as Rob fell into a restless sleep.

It was the same reoccurring nightmare that tormented him as a boy. There he was, a twelve-year-old kid at the corner mini-mart with his mother and father. They had just stopped in after church for a gallon of milk when two ski-masked men burst into the store.

"This is a robbery!" yelled the thug as he waved chrome-plated revolver in their faces. "Nobody move!" The second robber jumped over the counter and struck the clerk over the head with his gun, knocking him down and out. He then rummaged through the cash register taking all the bills and stuffed them into his pants' pockets.

"Give me your wallet!" ordered the thief as he thrust the gun into Rob's father's face.

"Give it to him, George!" pleaded his mother.

George started to reach for his wallet, but then hesitated. "You know what... No!" he said.

The explosion of the gun stunned everyone and they all stood motionless. George lay face down in a pool of his own blood, dead. The smell of gunpowder singed Rob's nostrils.

"George!" yelled Rob's mother as she instinctively reached out for her husband.

BOOM! A second shot rang out and Rob's mother clutched her chest. Blood oozed out from between her fingers and she collapsed beside her husband's lifeless body.

Rob was frozen. "Get down kid!" yelled the gunman, but he stood as if in defiance, staring at the gun that killed his parents and at the tattoo of a green and red serpent on the killer's forearm.

The other robber quickly jumped back over the counter and grabbed his accomplice by the arm. "Come on, man. Let's get out of here!" The two robbers ran from the store into the dark night, leaving Rob standing motionless, in a daze, staring over his dead parents.

Rob tossed, turned, and struggled to wake himself up from this familiar nightmare that was actually more than just a bad dream; it was a haunting memory of an all too real incident from his past. Rob awoke startled, gasping for breath, and shivering. " I'm gonna kill that guy... one way or another.... I'll find that monster and kill 'em," he vowed as he wiped the perspiration from his forehead and settled back down on his pillow.

The loud clash and clang of a metal tray being dropped by an orderly, sent a shockwave through Rob's body, and almost caused him to take cover under a nearby hospital bed. His heart pounded so hard that he thought it would come through his chest.

"Sorry, man," apologized the orderly. "Butter-fingers today," he added as he picked up the tray.

"Idiot!" yelled Rob. "You scared the crap out of me."

"I said I was sorry, man. Like I did it on purpose or something?"

"One more week and I'm outta here," declared Rob. "I'm going bananas in this place."

CHAPTER 3

Anticipation

Jenny left her tiny apartment in Huntington Beach and drove south on Pacific Coast Highway. The little, red, VW convertible weaved in and out of traffic as Jenny's long, blond hair waved in the breeze. The warm southern California sun, the smell of the ocean, and the wind in her face were exhilarating, but the little flutter she felt in her stomach brought her a different kind of excitement. She groped for the cell phone on the seat next to her; finally grasping it, she flipped it open with one hand.

"Mom, guess what?" she asked with bursting enthusiasm. "I just felt him move again. It's been going on for weeks, but I don't think I'll ever get used to it."

"Him? Are you sure it's a him?" chided Jenny's mother, Rose.

Rose believed she was also too young to be a grandmother. She liked it when strangers asked if she and Jenny were sisters. Her and her husband, Wally, divorced when Jenny was twelve years old due to his alcoholism. The untimely divorce brought Rose and Jenny closer together and strengthened their faith as it made them more reliant on God's provision and reliance in God. "Mom, it's freakin' me out!" exclaimed Jenny. "Oh my God, there it goes again," she laughed, as the baby's kick grew stronger. "Got to be a boy to kick like that," she added.

"You need to get off the cell phone and drive with two hands," warned Rose. "Hang up, I'll meet you at the Surfside Café."

"Okay… *Grandma*," chimed Jenny.

"Don't call me Grandma. I'm not a grandmother yet," said Rose.

"Hey, Proverbs 17:6 says, 'Children's children are a crown to the aged.'"

"Well I'm not 'the aged' yet!"

Jenny laughed, "I'm almost there, and I'm starving!"

The Seaside Café was a small eatery that was frequented by surfers and local beach bums. Its white and blue paint was blistered and bubbled by the sun. It had been a small surf-shack in the sixties, where Harry Moss first started his small, custom board shop. Now, decades later, it had been transformed into a small restaurant on the edge of the Pacific Ocean. Burgers and fish tacos were the only items on the menu, but were good enough to pack the house.

Rose sat at an outside table sipping on an ice-cold diet Pepsi, staring out across the sand at the breakers that pounded the shoreline. Her mind drifted out to sea with the tide. The sound of squealing tires brought her back to reality and she turned her head quickly to search for the source. The red VW bug skidded to a stop, then backed into the sole parking place directly in front of the café.

"I should have known," uttered Rose.

Jenny came bouncing over to Rose's table with a huge grin. "Had to get that parking spot," she said with a laugh.

"You know, you are going to kill yourself and that baby," said Rose pointing to Jenny's bulging belly.

"I'm careful," chimed Jenny. "Did you order yet?"

Rose shook her head. "You're going to give me gray hair."

"Well, you are going to be a grand—"

"Don't say it, Jen," warned Rose as the waiter approached their table.

The waiter was a well-tanned, twenty-year-old surfer, clad only in white Bermuda shorts, a soiled tank top and flip-flops. His hair was a tangled bunch of brown curls that cascaded onto his shoulders. A dark tan made his broad smile seem brighter.

"What can I get you girls today?" he asked, as he looked them both up and down with a Cheshire cat grin.

"My sister and I will have a hamburger, fries and diet Pepsi," smiled Rose.

The waiter jotted down the order on a small white pad. "You got it, ladies," he said as he turned and headed into the café.

"Sister?" asked Jenny with a smirk.

Rose threw her head back and laughed out loud. "Well, look at these legs. What do you think? Aren't these the legs of a 20 year old?"

"I think I'm going to have to keep you away from my husband when he gets home, that's what I think," stated Jenny.

"Speaking of Rob, when is he coming home?" inquired Rose.

"I'll be picking him up at Camp Pendleton next week."

"Is he all right?"

"Physically or mentally?" asked Jenny.

"Both," replied Rose as she scooted her chair closer to Jenny.

"Physically, his leg still bothers him a lot and he needs to continue with his therapy. Mentally, he seems fine. We're both optimistic about the future, with the baby coming and all."

"That's great, Jen. I'm sure everything will be fine."

"Ya, Rob wrote in his last letter that as soon as he gets discharged from the marines, he's gonna look for a new job, and then we can get on with our lives."

CHAPTER 4

Homecoming

Jenny nervously tapped the steering wheel as she sat waiting in the Camp Pendleton parking lot. The wind off the ocean messed up the hairdo she had spent all morning creating, but the wind felt good. In the distance she could see the new Marine recruits marching back and forth as the Drill Instructors barked out cadence. It wasn't that long ago that Rob was going through those same drills, but today he was coming home. It had been just over five months since she had seen her husband and he had never seen her pregnant.

Jenny thought back to the time when her and Rob first met. If there was such a thing as love at first sight, then she was definitely smitten when he walked into her high school Algebra class. When their eyes met, it was instant chemistry and neither one could wipe away the smiles on their faces. After class, he asked if he could walk her to her next period. She agreed, and he carried her books, stopping in front of her Journalism classroom, not caring that he was going to be late for his class, which was clear across campus. The very next weekend, Rob asked Jenny out on their first date. He arrived at her home in his father's blue Oldsmobile. Jenny thought that Rob appeared to be a little nervous meeting her mother for the first time, however, Jenny's mother put Rob at ease with her flirtatious behavior that embarrassed Jenny. She had spent most of Saturday morning picking out the dress she would wear. Finally, she settled on the new green one. When Rob saw her that evening, he said, "Wow! You look great!" He took her out to dinner at a beachside restaurant, but they hardly touched their food. They just talked and laughed until the waiter advised them that the restaurant was closing. He drove her home and walked her to the front door. "Can I kiss you goodnight?" he asked. She smiled, "I never kiss on the first date," she replied. He looked somewhat surprised by her answer, but nodded in acceptance. "I'll call you tomorrow," he stated. Jenny smiled and remembered that first date as though it had happened yesterday.

"I wonder if he'll think I look too fat or... ugly?" she said out loud. She looked down at her swollen stomach just as the baby inside her kicked. "Hey, that one hurt, little buddy," she said as she placed her hand on the spot. "Your Daddy's going to be here any minute. Be patient."

Jenny looked up to see Rob limping alone toward her across the parking lot. It wasn't one of those "Welcome Home Hero" receptions that they show on the evening news. There was no media, no military band, and no throngs of people to greet the few returning marines. The huge cargo plane had dropped Rob and a handful of other marines off at the end of the tarmac. He was dressed in dessert camouflage fatigues with a large duffel bag slung over his shoulder. He walked slowly with the aid of a black cane. The broad smile on his face changed to a wince every time his right foot landed on the asphalt.

Jenny stepped out of the car and ran across the parking lot. She threw her arms around his neck and passionately kissed him. They swayed in the embrace until they almost toppled over, then looked into each other's eyes, and started laughing out loud.

"I'm so glad you're home. I've been so worried about you! Are you all right?"

"I'm okay, honey. I'm so happy to be home," he said as he pulled back from their embrace. "Wow. Look at you. My lil' Mama! You look fantastic."

Rob placed his hand on Jenny's stomach, then again wrapped his arms around her, and kissed her intensely. He had only been gone a little over five months, but he was so glad to be able to hold her in his arms once again. The thought of being killed in battle, never seeing Jenny or their baby, weighed heavily on his emotions. Tears trickled down his cheeks.

The little red VW Bug hummed northward up the freeway toward Huntington Beach, dodging in and out of traffic.

"Slow down," warned Rob as he nervously squirmed in the passenger seat.

"I can't wait to get you home. My mom and I have been worried sick. We've all been praying for you, ya know."

"Yeah, thanks, honey. I'm lucky to be alive. I know everything's going to be great, with the baby coming and all."

"I know. We are so blessed. So, what are your plans? What do you want to do now that you are out of the Corps?"

"First thing Monday morning, I'm going down to the Unemployment Office to get a job," advised Rob. "Maybe, we should look for a bigger apartment."

"I'm so excited!" blurted out Jenny.

"Me too, me too… Wow… Did you ever think when we were in high school that we'd be married and having a baby?" asked Rob.

"Sure. I used to think about it everyday."

Rob chuckled, "It's just amazing. It's really good to be home, with you and… him," said Rob as he reached over and rubbed Jenny's tummy. "We've got a wonderful life ahead of us."

CHAPTER 5

The Unemployment Office

"Is this your first time?" asked a twenty year old Hispanic male dressed in a white t-shirt, blue jeans and brown work boots.

"Excuse me?" replied Rob. "My first—?"

"Your first time… at the Unemployment office."

"Oh, yeah,"

"I thought so. You look like you're lost, man. See, you got to take a number, fill out all these forms, and then sit and wait 'til they call you."

"Oh. Uh, thanks," said Rob as he pulled a number from the dispenser.

"You a Marine, right? One of those Semper Fi dudes, huh? I can tell."

"Ya. I just got back from Iraq."

"Got your leg messed up, huh? Too bad, man," he said as he extended his hand. "My name is David."

Rob shook David's hand, "Rob Jacobs. I'm a civilian now."

"There's a couple of seats in the back," David said pointing to the back of the crowded waiting room. The two squeezed past several people until they reached their seats and sat down.

"Let me tell you how to beat the system, dude," advised David. "The Man is always trying to screw the little guy out of what he's entitled to, you know?" David looked around the room and then scrutinized the people seated closest to him and Rob.

"Here's what you need to do to collect your unemployment checks," whispered David as he leaned closer to Rob's ear.

"I'm not here to collect. I'm here for a job," stated Rob. "I don't need to try to beat the system out of anything."

"Okay, fine, dude. But there's gonna be a day when you need the dough and they're gonna screw you out of it," advised David. "*Believe* me."

"David, I think they just called your number?" Rob stated as he pointed to the ticket in David's hand.

"Yeah, that's me," he said as he got up and squeezed between the chairs. "Good luck, man."

Rob looked around the waiting room at all the serious and sad faces. There was not a smile to be found inside the four gray walls. *Could all these people be out of work?*

He nervously tapped his foot while he flipped through several outdated magazines as the time dragged on.

"Number 21. Number 21," blurted out the loud speaker. Rob checked the number on his ticket. "Finally! My lucky number," he said as he made his way through the crowded waiting room to the designated window.

"Okay, Mr. Jacobs. You need to take your paperwork and meet with an employment counselor. Mrs. Jackson is your counselor. Just go through that door. She is waiting for you," said the clerk at the window.

Rob gathered up his forms and went through the door where he was met by Mrs. Jackson, a heavy set, black woman, about 40 years old, wearing a dark green dress with yellow flowers and a lime green sweater. Her reddish-colored wig was tilted a little too far forward, which gave the impression that her forehead was only an inch or so tall.

"Mr. Jacobs, I presume?" asked Mrs. Jackson as she motioned for Rob to take a seat.

"Yes, ma'am, Rob Jacobs."

"I see you just out of da military," she said looking at his paperwork. "What type of job you looking fo', Mr. Jacobs?"

"Well, I'll take just about anything. We've got a baby coming soon."

"Oh, dat's nice. Uh, Mr. Jacobs, I don't have anything available fo' you at dis time."

"You're kidding, right? I need a job. I can do anything."

"Sorry. Take these forms, fill dem out and continue looking fo' a job. I'll keep lookin', but no promises. A lot of people are out of work and not a lot of companies are hirin'."

"What you're really saying is that nobody's hiring people with only one good leg?"

"No, Mr. Jacobs, dat's not what I said. But you have to take into consideration dat you are limited to certain jobs because of your disability."

"Fine. Do you have anything at all?"

Mrs. Jackson looked through a stack of papers, pulled one out and faced Rob. "All there isa clerking position at a mini-mart."

"How much does it pay?"

"Uh, well, it only pays minimum wage, but… after you're there a month, they'll increase it a dollar."

"You are kidding me, right?" said a frustrated Rob. "I told you I have a baby coming, didn't I?"

"Dis is all I have fo' you, Mr. Jacobs."

"Okay, all right, I guess it will have to do." Mrs. Jackson handed Rob a piece of paper with the name, address and contact person at the mini-mart. Rob stared at it for a minute, then got up and left.

He went back to the apartment where Jenny was preparing lunch in the kitchen.

"Hey, honey. I'm home," he said as he flopped down onto the couch.

"How did it go? Did they have anything for you?" she asked bounding into the living room. She could see disappointment on his face and knew right away it didn't go well for Rob.

"Jenny, could you get me a glass of water and some of those pain pills in the cabinet? My leg is killing me."

Jenny went back into the kitchen, poured a glass of water and got Rob's painkillers. She returned to the living room and handed them to Rob who hurriedly gulped them down.

"Well, are you going to tell me if you got a job?" she asked.

"It's a minimum wage position at a mini-mart. A clerk or something," said Rob discouragingly.

"Don't worry, babe… just think of it as a stepping stone to something better," encouraged Jenny. "It's not like it's your life's career."

"You're right, Jen," he said. "You are always right. Bring that pregnant belly over here and give me a kiss." Jenny carefully leapt onto the couch, embraced Rob, and kissed him.

CHAPTER 6

Graveyard

The mini-mart was not located in the best part of town, but it was kept immaculate inside and out. "A diamond in the rough" locals would say. The several rows of merchandise were always stocked neatly on the shelves, and bottles of liquor were organized by brand and size behind the counter. The windows were cleaned daily, and the parking lot swept twice a day. There was never an iota of trash to be found. The owner, Mr. Patel, emigrated from India with his parents when he was just a boy, but he somehow managed to keep the old country accent. The neighborhood patrons of his mini-mart all agreed that the feisty Patel had a short-man complex. At five-foot even and a little over a hundred pounds, he ruled his mini-mart like a third world dictator. Employees and customers alike were often the subject of verbal abuse.

"Rob Jacobs. This is a very important job. A lot of responsibility. You will be working from midnight to eight in the morning. All by yourself. It gets pretty slow so you can do the sweeping up, wash the windows, stock the shelves, and clean the toilets and all that. I showed you how to use the cash register. Do you have any questions?" asked Mr. Patel adjusting his black, horn-rimmed glasses.

"No, sir. I think I got it. Thank you for the opportunity, sir."

Patel nodded in approval, handed Rob a broom and walked briskly out the front door, leaving Rob all alone in the store. He looked around at the totally empty mini-mart and began to sweep the floor. The longer he was on his feet, the more his leg throbbed like a pulsating pain beacon. He reached into his pocket, pulled out two painkillers and swallowed them without water. Boredom was setting in as he finished up cleaning the glass entry doors. At three in the morning his first customer, a sixteen-year-old boy, six feet tall, thin build, wearing a red hooded sweatshirt and blue jeans entered the store.

"Hi. Can you tell me what time it is? I'm supposed to be home by two," said the teen as he approached Rob who was standing behind the counter.

"Well, you're an hour late."

"Thanks. I wasn't going to buy anything, but I guess I'll have a pack of gum," he said as he picked out a pack of gum from the rack and put a dollar on the counter.

Rob rang it up on the cash register and gave him the change. "Anything else?"

The teenager shook his head, turned and left the store. Rob looked at the clock on the wall. "This has got to be the most boring job in the world," he said out loud. He then restocked the shelves. He checked the big wall clock again, and again.

Finally, at 8 o'clock sharp his replacement, Jodie Welker, entered the store. Jodie was a chunky white female in her early thirties with long, dark-brown hair that reached her black patent leather belt. As soon as she walked in, things began to get busy as customers on their way to work filtered through the front door.

"Excuse me, Rob is it? Did you make the coffee?"

"Oh, no. I didn't know I was supposed to make it."

Jodie shook her head and gave Rob a disgusted look. "It's hard to find good help these days."

Rob ignored her remark and left the mini-mart. The brightness of the morning sun made it difficult for Rob to keep his eyes open. He managed to walk the five blocks to his home. By the time he reached the front door the pain in his leg had radiated all the way up to his hip. He was surprised to see Jenny seated at the kitchen table sipping a cup of coffee.

"Hey Hon. How was your first night on the job?"

"Boring. I only had one customer all night long and that was for a pack of gum. All I did was clean up all night. Floors, windows, toilets."

Jenny got up, walked over to Rob and put her arms around his neck. "I'm sorry honey. Maybe it was just a slow night? I'm sure it will get better."

"Yeah, I don't think it could get any worse," he said as he kicked off his shoes, removed his shirt and headed for the bedroom.

"Don't you want me to fix you some breakfast?"

"No, I'm going to bed," yawned Rob. "Thanks anyway, honey."

"Want some company?"

Rob smiled and gave his head a nod in the direction of the bedroom.

Only two hours had past since Rob fell dead asleep and he was awoken by a jolt of pain down his leg. He rolled over at looked at an angelic Jenny sound asleep next to him. Quietly, he slithered out from under the sheet and made his way into the bathroom where he opened the medicine cabinet and took the bottle of pain medication. He poured himself a glass of water from the tap and swallowed some pills straight from the bottle. Rob looked at himself in the mirror, but he did not recognize the person in the reflection. Was it that this person looked older? Tired? Or just in pain? Worried perhaps? Concerned about the future— his job, his marriage, and the baby? Rob slipped back into bed so as to not wake Jenny. He just lay there and watched her sleep until she opened her eyes two hours later.

"You should be asleep," she whispered. "Did you have a bad dream again?"

"No, my leg is killing me."

"You really need to get some sleep."

"I'll try," he said as he rolled over and closed his eyes.

He slept for a few hours until the pain medication wore off, but he had the same recurring nightmare, and was almost relieved to be awake, except for the pain. He reached for Jenny but discovered she had left the bed. He got up, took a shower, shaved and got dressed.

Jenny had made some dinner for the two of them and set the table in the kitchen. "I made your favorite," she exclaimed. "Salad, steak and a baked potato, with peach cobbler for dessert."

"Are you trying to make me as round as you?" he laughed.

"Just for that remark, you are doing the dishes Mister," she playfully scolded.

After dinner, Rob did help Jenny with the dishes. They took turns splashing soapsuds on each other and laughed like a couple of school kids. When it was time for him to leave for work, he gave her a big, but gentle hug.

"I don't know how much longer I will be able to do this," he said.

"Do what?"

"Hug you. This belly is getting pretty big, you know," he laughed.

"It's time for you to go," she said unamused.

"I hope tonight is better than last night."

"I'm sure it will be," encouraged Jenny.

Rob left the car for Jenny in case of an emergency and walked the five blocks to the mini-mart. His leg bothered him every step of the way, but he refused to use the military issued cane. The longer he walked the more pronounced his limp became.

—

Time dragged on the graveyard shift. The nights turned to weeks, but it felt more like years to Rob. However, it gave him plenty of time to daydream about the birth of his child. This night would prove to be busier than most because the first customer came in to the store at two in the morning and interrupted Robs sweeping of the floors. The middle age, heavy-set, black man wearing a tan jacket, khaki pants and a black watch cap briskly walked straight to the counter. Rob hobbled back behind the counter and flashed a smile, welcoming his first customer. "How ya doin'? Can I help you?"

"Yeah, you can give me all the money in the cash register, now!" the man demanded as he pulled a blue steel revolver from under his tan jacket and thrust it into Rob's face.

Rob froze as he was overwhelmed by a flood of emotions. The vision of the gunman who killed his parents flashed in his memory like a strobe light. It was his recurring nightmare, although this time it was once again real.

"I said NOW! What are you some kind of retard?"

"Okay, okay. Just relax. I'm getting you your money right now."

Rob opened the cash register, placed all the cash in a brown paper bag, and handed it to the crook who put the paper bag into his jacket pocket, reached across the counter and pulled Rob toward him by his collar. He struck him over the head with the barrel of the gun. Rob saw flashes like exploding artillery and he fell to the floor.

"Don't try to stop me! And, don't call the cops or I'll come back and—" he growled as he turned and ran from the mini-mart, disappearing into the darkness.

Rob, dazed and groggy, struggled to get to his feet. He reached for the phone and dialed 9-1-1. After two rings the police dispatcher answered, "9-1-1. What's your emergency?"

"I've just been robbed. Patel's Mini-mart. The guy just left, he had a gun."

"Sir, are you all right? Do you need an ambulance?"

"No, I think I'm okay. He ran north on 3rd Street. A big, heavy-set, black guy, wearing a tan jacket and tan pants."

"That's 4353 S. 3rd Street, Patel's Mini-mart. The police are on the way, sir. Just stay on the phone with me until they arrive. Don't hang up."

"I need to... call my boss."

"Wait for the police, sir."

Rob, still groggy, hung up the phone and dialed Mr. Patel's home phone. Patel answered after four rings.

"Hello," yawned Patel.

"Mr. Patel, it's Rob down at the store."

"Rob? Rob, it's after two in the morning—"

"I just got robbed. Some guy with a gun. He—"

"I'll be right there," stated Patel. "Did you call the police?"

"The cops just now got here."

Rob heard the sound of Mr. Patel's phone being slammed down on the receiver.

Patel hurriedly put on his gray sweat pants, a black hooded sweatshirt and a pair of K-Swiss tennis shoes. He accidentally bumped into the dresser and woke up his wife, Lily, a 35-year-old raven-haired Indian woman originally from Calcutta.

"What's wrong?" she asked.

"We got robbed, again."

Patel raced to the mini-mart, ran past an officer outside the front door and interrupted Rob as he was talking to a policeman.

"Rob! What happened? Did they take all my money?"

"He hit me on the head with his gun and—"

"Did he get all the money?"

"Yeah, everything."

"Didn't you try to stop him? You're a big shot war hero. You didn't do anything?"

"He had a gun."

The police officer looked at Patel in amazement as though he could not believe what he was hearing. All this guy cares about is his money. "Excuse me, Mr. Jacobs, I need your signature on this report," said the officer as he stepped between Rob and Patel.

"Is that all, officer?" asked Rob.

"Yes, thanks. The detectives will be in touch," he advised as he turned and looked at Patel. "Sorry, Jacobs," he added as he shook his head and walked out of the mini-mart.

"Why didn't you try to stop the robber?" questioned Patel.

"Stop the robber? The guy had a gun. He hit me right here," pointing to a laceration and lump on the left side of his forehead.

"Maybe you got some of my money too? Huh, Rob? Maybe you were in on it?"

"What?! How dare you!" said Rob as his face grew red and his jaw tightened. "I work my butt off for you… and this is the thanks I get? You can have this job. I quit!"

Rob stormed out of the store. He had walked a whole block without noticing the pain in his leg. When he slowed his pace and cooled down, the pain shot through his leg like repeated lightning strikes. Limping heavily, he finally arrived at his apartment to find Jenny sleeping on the living room couch.

Jenny awoke to the noise in the kitchen and went to investigate only to find Rob rummaging through the cabinet drawers. "Rob, you're home early. Is everything all right?"

"Yeah, everything's fine, or at least it will be. Where are those pills?"

"Rob, what happened to your head? You're bleeding!"

"I got robbed tonight."

"Oh my God! Are you all right?"

"I'm okay. But that jerk, Patel, accused me of being part of the robbery."

"What?! You can't be serious."

"I just quit. Walked out."

"I don't blame you. How could he—"

"It'll be okay," he said as he held Jenny in his arms. "I'll find another job. A better one. Don't worry," he added trying to comfort her.

"I'm not worried," she said sternly, pulling back from their embrace. She stared at him for a moment. "Rob, you're hurt. Let me put something on that cut."

"It's nothing. I'm going to the VA Hospital tomorrow. I'll have 'em take a look at it then. I'm fine."

CHAPTER 7

The VA Hospital

Jenny drove the little VW Bug down Seventh Street toward the VA Hospital while Rob rode shotgun taking in the sights. The ten-story building loomed in the distance like a big, white elephant. From a distance, Rob could see a few palm trees around the building, but as they got closer he noticed that the flag was at half-mast. Jenny dropped him off in front of the building and drove around the parking lot. After finding a place to park, she made her way inside the hospital and to the information desk where she was told to have a seat in the waiting room. Rob had been directed to the fourth floor where a nurse led him to an examining room. "The doctor will be with you in a few minutes," she said. "Take off your clothes, put this gown on and have a seat on the table."

Rob sat patiently on the examining table in a small room at the Long Beach VA Hospital reading the health charts on the walls. It was his first time at the hospital since returning from Iraq and he was hopeful that they would be able to relieve some of his pain.

Doctor Wang, a 54 year old Chinese-American, about five and a half feet tall, medium build, wearing a white coat entered the room reading Rob's medical chart through thick, round, out-dated glasses.

"Corporal Jacobs," said the doctor as he flashed a wide, enthusiastic smile. "It looks like you've been through a lot."

"Yes, I guess you can say that, Doc."

Doctor Wang set the chart down on the examining table with a concerned look on his face. "Well, what do we have here?" he said as he touched Rob's forehead with both hands. "That's quite a contusion you have there. How did you do that?"

"Ouch," cried Rob as he pulled back from the doctor's touch. "I got robbed and the jerk hit me on the head with his gun."

"Did you lose consciousness?"

"No, I don't think so, but I might have momentarily. It really doesn't bother me, but my leg is killing me. Can you give me some pain medication?"

"Lay back on the table and let me take a look at that leg."

Rob lay down on the table and adjusted his hospital gown. He stared up at the fluorescent lights on the ceiling and tried to relax.

Doctor Wang placed his left hand on Rob's knee and his right hand on Rob's ankle and squeezed ever so slightly. "Screws, bolts, metal rods and plates. The surgeon did a wonderful job putting you back together," he marveled. "It's a miracle he saved this leg."

"Ouch," hollered Rob. "That hurts, doc."

"Here? Does it hurt when I do this?" he asked as he squeezed Rob's calf.

Rob almost levitated off of the table and his face turned as red as a fire truck. "Owwww!" he bellowed. "What are you doing? I told you how much pain I have there!"

"Sorry, Corporal, but I have to examine you."

"Just don't kill me, doc," Rob said sternly.

"You appear to be healing fine and everything seems to be okay. As for the pain, you're just going to have to live with it."

"Live with it? Huh? Can't you just give me a stronger dose of meds or something?"

"Your chart shows that you are already at the maximum dosage. I can't increase it."

Rob grabbed his leg and writhed in pain. "Look, doc, I'm really trying to be strong here, but it's getting to be more that I can deal with."

"Perhaps, a visit with the hospital psychiatrist would help?"

"What?! Do you think I'm imagining this? Come on, doc!?"

Dr. Wang stared at him, brows pinched. He sighed. "Okay, Mr. Jacobs. I'm going to write you a new prescription for the pain, but I must warn you that they are highly addictive. Use them sparingly, and the goal is to wean yourself off of them soon," warned Doctor Wang. "You can get dressed now. See the nurse at the counter. She'll have your prescription."

Downstairs in the crowded waiting room, Jenny looked around at a hundred disabled and injured vets. An elderly couple held hands and looked as though they were both in a trance. The white-haired old man looked up at his wife with a loving smile, and then he adjusted his cap that read "Pearl Harbor Survivor." *There are a lot of survivors in this waiting room*, thought Jenny, and she said a silent prayer for them.

"Let's go," said Rob, who startled Jenny, deep in prayer.

"Oh, your scared me. I didn't expect you back so soon."

"Come on, let's get out of here," he said anxiously. "This place creeps me out."

"What did the doctor say? Are they going to operate on your leg again?"

"He wanted to send me to a shrink. Can you imagine? I guess he thinks it's all in my head? Let's go. I've got to fill this prescription."

Jenny took Rob's hand and they walked slowly to the massive parking lot. Finally, they reached the little Volkswagen convertible bug. "It's such a nice day, do we want to put the top down?" she asked.

"No. Just stop at the liquor store on the way home."

"For What?" Jenny questioned.

"I want to buy a six pack," Rob said curtly.

"Of what? Beer? Since when do you drink?" inquired Jenny. "You know, I don't think you should be mixing beer with those pills?"

"Don't worry about it."

"The combination could give you a heart attack or something."

"Just stop at the store, okay?" Rob snapped.

Jenny became tight jawed and sullen. She drove to the store without saying a word and pulled up in the parking lot. "Rob, will you pray with me?"

Rob took a deep breath. He knew of Jenny's steadfast faith and her question made him see that his faith seemed to be slipping away. "Sure, honey. Look, Jen, don't worry. I... I'm sorry. I—"

Jenny reached out and took Rob by the hand before he could say another word.

"Dear Lord, please protect our marriage, heal Rob's leg, and bless our baby boy. Amen"

"Boy? So you think it's a boy, huh?"

"I just know it. I think a mother knows these things."

Rob laughed, leaned over and kissed Jenny on the cheek. "I love you, you know?" he said without expecting an answer. "Let's go home. Forget the beer."

CHAPTER 8

The Search

Sweat dripped from Rob's brow and splattered on the sidewalk like a summer rain. He walked in the shadows of the buildings to keep cooler, but the sun's heat radiated off the cement like a giant pizza oven. "Sorry, but things are kind of slow right now," echoed from business after business. "Come back in a couple of weeks. Things might pick up by then."

Rob limped along, stopping from time to time to look into the storefront windows. *I'd like to buy that for Jenny and the baby,* he thought. *Too bad I'm broke and jobless! I can't even buy a cold drink!* He continued on for another hour in the hot afternoon sun; his leg pulsated with pain. Discouraged, he walked home.

Jenny was busy in the kitchen preparing dinner when she heard the front door open, and then slam shut. She put down the head of lettuce and walked into the living room where Rob had plopped down on the couch.

"You look like you had a hard day. Any luck?"

"No, same old thing. Come back in a couple of weeks. Maybe tomorrow will be better."

"I hope you're hungry?" asked Jenny. "I made your favorite, tacos."

"Sounds good. I am hungry, and... thirsty."

"Ten minutes. Give me ten minutes, honey."

Jenny finished cooking and poured two big glasses of ice tea. She put the food and the drinks on a tray and carried them into the living room. She was somewhat surprised to see Rob fast asleep on the couch. Setting the tray down on the coffee table, she went over and kissed him on the forehead. "Time to eat," she chimed softly, hating to wake him.

"Oh," he said opening his eyes. "I must have dozed off." He sat up, grabbed the ice tea and guzzled it down without stopping. "I'm thirsty," he announced. Jenny laughed.

"I'm starving too," he exclaimed reaching for a plate of tacos.

"Why don't you say grace, Rob?"

Rob had been saying grace for their meals since they were dating. He considered it an honor and a blessing to give thanks to his God. And, that was one of the things that Jenny loved about him. He seemed to be forgetting lately though.

"Sure, Jenny, I'll say grace," agreed Rob. "Thank you, father God, for my lovely wife and baby. Thank you for saving me, and for bringing me safely home. Thank you for everything and bless our food for the nourishment of our bodies, and Lord, please help me find a job. In Christ's name. Amen."

Rob and Jenny smiled at each other as Jen patted Rob on the hand. After their meal Rob helped Jenny wash and dry the dishes. His spirits raised, he kissed his wife on the forehead. "I'm off to take a shower and hit the sack. Got to get out there and hit the bricks again tomorrow."

"I know God has got something good in store for you," she said. "Romans 8:28, 'And we know that all things work together for good to those who love God, to those who are called according to His purpose.'"

"Thanks Jen."

But, the rest of the week proved fruitless for his job search and on Friday a sort of hopelessness started to sink in, which was the beginning of Rob's depression.

Monday morning, Rob was slow to rise and get dressed. He felt he had almost exhausted the businesses within walking distance of his home and finding a job was not going to be as easy as he had hoped. The baby would be arriving in almost four months, which added to the urgency of finding work.

Just as he was leaving the house the phone rang. Jenny answered it. "Hello?" she said.

"Hello, this is Mrs. Jackson from the Unemployment Office calling for Rob Jacobs."

"Oh, yes, this is his wife. He was just about to go out the door, looking for work," she said as she motioned for Rob to take the phone.

"This is Rob Jacobs, can I help you?"

"Mr. Jacobs, I'm glad I got a hold of you. There is an opening at B & B Electronics. If you're interested, I can give you a name and phone number to set up an interview?"

"Yes, that's terrific."

"Now, Mr. Jacobs, you can't just go walkin' out on a job like you did at the mini-mart. You ain't entitled to unemployment benefits if you up and quit this job. Ya hear me?"

"Yes, ma'am, I know."

Rob scribbled down the information from Mrs. Jackson and hung up the phone. He looked at the sheet of paper for a long minute, and then jumped up and ran into the kitchen where Jenny was washing dishes.

"Well, what did she say?" asked Jenny as she flung the dishtowel over her shoulder.

"I need to call and make an appointment to see this guy at B&B Electronics. I think I have a good shot at getting this job."

"Great! Did she say how much the job pays?"

"I haven't been hired yet. It's just an interview," he added and turned to walk back to the living room.

"I know, I know. But I've been praying God would give you the right job and—"

"Yeah, maybe it will turn out to be something good." Rob walked into the bathroom and stared at himself in the mirror. He reached into his pocket and pulled out a vial of pain pills, popped the cap and poured a couple into his hand. He stared at them for a few minutes, and then tossed them into his mouth and swallowed them with a handful of water. Rob was not sure if he liked the reflection in the mirror.

CHAPTER 9

A New Job

Bright and early the next morning Rob stood out front of the B &
B Electronics Store and looked up at the sign over the door. He had
walked past the business almost everyday, but had never thought
about working there. Through the front door he could see a seventy-
year-old man standing behind the glass counter. The man was rather
short and stocky, with a crop of thick, snow-white hair. He wore
a pair of gold wire-rimmed glasses, a blue long-sleeved shirt, dark
pants and a tan apron with two large pockets.

Rob was the first person to walk through the front door and
noticed he was alone with the old man behind the counter.

"Excuse me, sir. Can you tell me where I might find Mr. Werner?"
asked Rob.

"You must be Rob Jacobs? I'm Mr. Werner, but you can call me
Felix," he advised in a thick German accent.

"I understand that you might have an opening for a clerk?"

"Come on back here to my office," said Felix as he motioned
Rob to follow him. "The lady at the unemployment office said that
you're an ex-marine. Wounded?"

"Yes, sir. I injured my leg."

"I have a lot of respect for soldiers, like yourself. My son was a
marine, you know. He was killed in Viet Nam. You kinda remind

me of him," he said as he took out his wallet and removed an old photograph of his son and showed it to Rob.

"I'm sorry for your loss, sir."

"My son was a hero, you know. His squad was ambushed in the jungle and he held off the enemy until everyone escaped. He posthumously won the Medal of Valor. He was a real hero," said Felix tearfully as he put the photograph back into his wallet.

"Yes, he was… a real hero," said Rob.

"Of course, you wouldn't have to lift anything too heavy. Small electronics stuff, you know?" he said changing the subject as he wiped a tear from underneath his glasses. "I can't afford to pay you too much, but it is more than minimum wage. A chance for advancement! Ya know, I'll be looking for a manager down the road. When can you start?"

"Wow, well, uh, I can start right now!"

"Ha, ha," laughed Felix. "How about if you take these papers home, fill them out and come in at eight tomorrow morning?" Felix handed Rob an application. "Here, it's for tax and medical insurance. Bring these back tomorrow."

"Thank you, Mr. Werner, sir. I really appreciate the opportunity. I won't let you down, sir."

"Call me Felix."

Rob excitedly took the paperwork and hurriedly left the store. He walked home briskly, barely noticing the pain in his leg. Jenny was sitting on the couch knitting a baby outfit when Rob burst through the front door waiving the job application.

"Honey, I got the job. I start tomorrow. It's more than minimum wage and there are benefits too!"

"That's great! Didn't I tell you?"

"We should celebrate. Champagne."

"Champagne? Did you forget that I'm pregnant?"

"Oh, yeah, uh, I guess I got a little carried away, huh?" Rob chuckled.

He walked over to Jenny, bent over and kissed her on the forehead.

The news bulletin on the television interrupted the moment. A stoic news anchor reported that the day's recent bombing attack in Baghdad might bring about an abrupt end to the war. Images of Iraqi tanks being destroyed by U.S. missiles flashed across the screen. Rob subconsciously rubbed his injured right leg. The good news about his new job was dampened when the flashbacks of combat flooded over him like a broken levy. The image of his good friend and comrade-in-arms, Manny Garcia, laying dead his arms burned in his brain.

CHAPTER 10

A Turn for the Worst

Felix Werner rose ten minutes before his alarm clock sounded, which was his daily habit. He quickly dressed and made a pot of tea as Miss Kitty, his blue-eyed Siamese cat brushed up against his pant leg. "Yes, I know. You want some milk, don't you?" After pouring a small bowl of milk for the cat, he sat down at the small kitchen table with a cup of tea and surveyed the tiny one bedroom apartment. His eyes came to rest on the pictures of his deceased wife and son and he was momentarily transported back to fond memories of the past. The meowing of Miss Kitty brought him back to the present. "Yes, I know. It's time for me to go to work. Now, you take care of the apartment while I'm gone," he said as he locked the door on his way out.

After a short drive to work, he parked the old Ford Edsel in the alley behind the business as usual, and entered through the back door. "Another day, another dollar," he muttered. Felix shuffled out of the back office and made his way between several open boxes of electronic components to the front counter. Later that morning he watched with the admiration of a father as Rob made his third sale of the day. After the customer left, Felix approached Rob and put his age-spotted hand on Rob's shoulder.

"You gotta minute, Rob?"

"Sure, Mr. Werner. Is there something you'd like me to do?"

"No, Rob. I just want to say that you've been here over a month now and… well, you are doing a really great job."

"Thank you, sir. I—"

"I'm going to give you a raise. It's not much, but I always say… every little bit helps," he laughed.

"Thank you. I appreciate that, Mr. Werner. "Felix. Call me Felix."

Later in the evening, Felix removed the day's receipts from the cash register, placed them in a cloth bank bag and walked toward his office. He glanced over his shoulder and observed Rob sweeping up with a broom.

"Rob, I'm leaving now. Can you lock up?"

"No problem. Go ahead. See you tomorrow."

Felix left the building through the back door as usual. The tan cloth bank bag clutched tightly in his hand, he walked through the dark alley behind the store to his prized 1958 Ford Edsel.

Rob locked the front door, surveyed the room and noticed that some merchandise had fallen from the top shelf and landed on the aisle. After getting a ladder from the back room, he gathered up the items, climbed the ladder and replaced them on the top shelf. As he started to climb down, his right foot slipped off the rung and he toppled to the floor with a resounding thud. Rob grabbed his leg as pain shot through it like a lightning bolt. He reached into his pocket and removed a vial of pain pills. He popped the cap with his thumb and attempted to pour some directly into his mouth, but the vial was empty. After lying there a few minutes, he finished cleaning the store, made sure everything was locked and started the walk home. The pain was so intense that it brought tears to his eyes. He had only gone one block before he had to stop. He hoped the pain would lessen, but it did not. Rob could hear the music coming from Molly's Tavern and thought maybe just one beer would take the edge off the ache in his leg. After all, what would one drink hurt?

Unfortunately, this one drink was to become a nightly ritual and coupled with the pain medication, it became a deadly combination.

CHAPTER 11

Temptation

Felix Werner, stood behind the counter and nervously looked at the large clock on the wall. "This is not like Rob. Two hours late?" he said out loud as he picked up the telephone and dialed Rob's home phone. After one ring, Jenny answered.

"Hello, this is Felix Werner, from B & B Electronics. I wonder if I could speak to Rob? Is he there?"

"Oh, hi, Mr. Werner. I thought he told you? He went to the VA Hospital this morning. His leg was hurting real bad. I thought he called you?"

"No, he didn't call in. Is he okay?"

"I'm sorry. Yes, he's... well, I am worried about him Mr. Werner. He's been in a lot of pain, and the pills just aren't enough anymore. I think that's why he started drinking and that's gotten worse too. He's just turning into a different person."

Felix noticed the tension, concern and worry in Jenny's voice, but he was not sure how to console her.

"I am so sorry. I had no idea what Rob has been going through. I will talk to him."

"Oh, no, you can't," she warned. "Rob is a proud man. He'd be upset with me for telling you. Besides, you don't need to make this your problem."

"Oh, it's no problem. Rob reminds me so much of my son, Paul. And, you are like the wife Paul never had. Okay? Don't worry. Everything will be all right," he assured her as he hung up the phone and stared at the ceiling.

—

The large waiting room at the Long Beach Veteran's Hospital was jammed packed like a can of sardines. Rob managed to find the last available chair after he checked in with the receptionist. *There must be veterans here from the last four wars*, he thought. World War II, Korea, Viet Nam, and the Persian Gulf veterans lined the walls, some with injuries far greater than Rob had endured; however, no one could see the damage done inside their heads. The doctors had told Rob that in addition to his leg injury, he also suffered from Post Traumatic Stress Disorder, which was a common malady of war veterans. PTSD originated from exposure to combat situations and was a major cause of depression, as well as drug and alcohol abuse in returning soldiers. Rob was just one of the reported 62% of soldiers returning from the Persian Gulf War who suffered from PTSD.

The automatic doors flew open and a middle-aged man in a wheel chair rolled into the waiting room. His long brown wavy hair was windblown and unkempt. It looked as though he hadn't shaved or showered in a couple of weeks. Under the brown leather jacket with holes in the sleeves was a once white t-shirt with several unidentifiable stains. Nobody seemed to notice his attire or unclean appearance, but their eyes couldn't help but gravitate toward the stumps that ended at his knees. After signing in, his strong, hairy hands rolled the wheels that came to an abrupt halt in front of Rob's chair.

"Marine, right? Semper Fidelis, man. How ya doin'?" he said and extended his hand to Rob. Rob did not respond, but looked away toward the reception desk.

"Oh, I get it. You're too good to talk to me? Is that it?" he queried. "Or maybe you're offended at a man with no legs, huh?"

"No man, it's nothing like that. Uh, my name's Rob, Rob Jacobs."

"Lenny Lomax. That's Sergeant Leonard T. Lomax, United States Army. But you can call me Lenny. Stepped on a friggin' land mine in Kuwait. Got a metal plate right here," he said pointing to the side of his head. You could not tell by looking at him, but Lomax was in fact a hero. Sgt. Lomax led his squad through the oil fields in Kuwait where they were ambushed by Iraqi forces. Several of his men were wounded, but they drove the enemy back across the border. Lomax picked up a young soldier that had been seriously wounded and carried him to safety on his shoulders, only to step on a land mine and lose both legs in the process. Sgt. Lomax, for his acts of heroism on the battlefield, received the Purple Heart and the Medal of Valor.

Rob nodded and forced a crooked smile as Lenny extended his hand once again. Rob shook his hand and offered a weak, "Sorry, man."

"Don't be sorry for me, dude. There's a lot of guys got it worse off."

"Yeah, you're right. I lost one of my buddies in Iraq."

"Ha! He was one of the lucky ones," Lenny said sarcastically. "What are you here for, anyway? You look okay to me."

"Outta painkillers… for my leg. And, I've been having these headaches lately."

Lenny leaned over toward Rob and whispered into his ear, "That stuff they give you for pain ain't no good. I got some real good pain meds, better than morphine."

"What do you mean?" asked Rob.

"You got something to write with? I'll give you my address and phone number. Just call me or come by and I'll hook you up."

Rob handed Lenny a pen and he wrote down his name and phone number on the inside of a match cover and handed it back to Rob.

"Uh, I'm not so sure… if I… well, okay, thanks man. I just might be in touch," added Rob hesitantly.

Lenny nodded and turned his wheelchair back towards the receptionist. "Cool."

CHAPTER 12

Choices

The morning sun was peaking over the rooftops when Felix parked his vintage Ford Edsel in the alley behind his shop. He took a deep breath, looked at the clear blue sky and walked briskly to the back door. Once inside, he took a quick look around. Everything seemed to be in order. He flipped around the "open sign" and unlocked the door. "We're in business!" he cheerfully exclaimed out loud.

Rob entered through the front door before Felix could make it to the sales counter.

"Good morning, Mr. Werner."

"Well, good morning to you. Are you all right?"

"I'm sorry I didn't call you yesterday," he said apologetically. "My leg, you know," he stated.

"Yes, I spoke to your wife, Jenny, on the phone."

"She told me that you called. You know these pregnant women; they get all emotional about stuff and blow things outta proportion."

"If there's anything I can do—"

"Well, actually, I was hoping to make a little extra money."

Felix looked around the store. He surveyed the shelves, the condition of the walls and then gazed up at the ceiling. "Hmm," he hummed. "Well, there are some things that could be done around the store. I could pay you a little extra if—"

"Thanks, but you don't have to create extra stuff for me to do," interrupted Rob. "I'll work it out."

"This place could use a new coat of paint and the shelves need to be reorganized," informed Felix. "Maybe you could come in on a Sunday when we're closed, or maybe stay late a few times a week?"

"Okay, sir. I can do that. Thank you."

"Rob, call me Felix," he advised with a cheesy grin. "Oh, and believe me, you are going to earn it, son."

—

Jenny tuned off the vacuum cleaner, stood up straight and stretched. She wasn't sure if the ache she felt in her lower back was from the housework or from all the baby-weight her stomach carried. She sighed a faint moan as a loud knock shook the front door.

"Who could that be at this time of day?" she wondered out loud as she walked to open the front door.

"Hello, Jenny. I was at the grocery store shopping and I was thinking about you, Rob and the… baby," the man said glancing down at her huge stomach. "So, I brought you some groceries. Oh, by the way, my name is—"

"Mr. Werner. I would know that accent anywhere. But, you didn't have to do that. You shouldn't have," she opined. "Please, come in. I was just cleaning."

"Oh, I can't come in. I've got some errands to run. Got to go. God bless you."

"Thank you, Mr. Werner. I appreciate all that you have done for us."

Jenny took the bag of groceries from Felix, placed it on the kitchen counter and returned to the front door to discover that Felix had disappeared down the hallway. She smiled.

—

The sun had set a few hours after closing time and Rob was still at the store. He gathered up the paint cans, brushes and rollers and put them in the back storage room. He checked the lock on the front door and exited the rear door, locking it with the deadbolt. He limped noticeably out of the dark alley and down the street toward home, but he hadn't gone a block when his leg throbbed with an excruciating pain. As he reached into his jacket pocket with his right hand he felt the book of matches that Lenny had given him. He examined it closely and read Lenny's address and phone number. "I don't know if I should call this guy?" he whispered to himself. As he stuck his left hand in his jacket pocket it automatically wrapped around his black plastic cell phone. He pulled it out and stared at it for a minute as he walked along. There was another jolt of pain that radiated through his whole leg and made him come to an abrupt halt on the sidewalk. He studied Lenny's number and then dialed.

"Hi, is this Lenny? This is Rob. I, uh—"

"Rob? Rob, who? I don't know anyone named Rob."

"You know, Rob from the VA Hospital? The marine."

"Oh, yeah, Rob. The jarhead. So, what's up man?"

"You said you could help me out… with my pain? Well, where can I meet you?"

"You got my address, right? Just come over."

"Okay, I'll see you in about a half an hour. I'm walkin' because my wife needs the car."

Rob hobbled the several blocks to the address on the matchbook. The old Marine Corps marching cadence sounded in his head every step of the way. Every so often he would say it out loud, "Hup, one, two, three, four…" It was something that helped him not think about the aches, pains and combat in Iraq. Rob noticed that in the last block or so the neighborhood had deteriorated. There were rundown apartment buildings that had not been painted in years. Trash was strewn on the sidewalk and in the gutters, and several homeless men slept in the doorways. He finally reached the front of Lenny's duplex and stood out front, staring at the front door. A conflict brewed inside of him, whether knock or just go home; however, it was the ache that started in his leg and traveled throughout his whole being that won the battle and made him forget all about home. Rob approached the dark-green, metal door and looked around for the source of the stench that had seized his nostrils. "Garbage," he said.

"Well, well, well. Look what the cat dragged in… Ha, ha," laughed Lenny as he was wheeled down the sidewalk toward his duplex by a skinny, thirty-something-year old, hunched over man with a protruding Adam's apple. "This is Icky," Lenny said, introducing his helper. "You guessed it. It's short for Icabod," he chuckled. "You know, like Icabod Crane."

"How ya doin', Lenny?" asked Rob.

"How do I look? You don't have to answer that. So, you looked me up for a little taste, eh?"

Lenny held out his hand and Rob reluctantly shook it.

"Well, I don't have very much money," said Rob as he reached into his pants pocket.

"Whoa, hey man, don't do that out here," demanded Lenny as he looked nervously up and down the street. "Wheel me up to my pad."

Rob grabbed the handles of the wheelchair and pushed Lenny up to his front door. Lenny fumbled for the keys, leaned forward and unlocked the door. "Push," ordered Lenny.

The small apartment looked as though a tornado had swept through it. There were dark green plastic bags overflowing with trash piled up in the living and the tiny kitchen. In the sink, dirty dishes were stacked a foot high and they looked like they had been there for quite some time. A can of roach spray was on the counter and two empty cans were on the kitchen floor.

"You live alone here?" inquired Rob.

"Yeah, my old lady left me a month or so ago. She said I wasn't the same person who went to the Gulf," grumbled Lenny. "Ha! No kiddin'! I ain't got no freakin' legs NOW. HA."

"Sorry about that, man. I, uh, got to get home. My wife's having a baby any day now."

Lenny wheeled himself into the kitchen and opened a cabinet drawer. He removed something wrapped in a black velvet cloth.

"Okay, man. I understand," said Lenny. "Look, here, take this," he added as he handed Rob the item wrapped in the black velvet cloth.

Rob slowly unwrapped it and found a syringe, a spoon, a half-empty book of matches and a small clear plastic baggie containing black tar heroin.

"A gift… from me to a fellow Gulf War vet," smiled Lenny. "You know how to use it, right?" he asked, and then noticed a puzzled look on Rob's face. "Look, you put this in the spoon, take a match, cook it. Take the syringe, draw some up… and BINGO. Got to get it in the vein though."

"Oh, uh, okay, how much do I owe you?" asked Rob hesitantly as he fumbled through his pockets looking for money that was not there.

"Hey, no. no… now don't do that, man. No… it's free, a gift," grinned Lenny.

"Really? Okay, cool, thanks. I got to get going. Thanks, Lenny, you're a life saver."

Lenny nodded in approval as Rob placed the black velvet cloth containing the illegal items into his jacket pocket and left the apartment. Paranoia set in as he walked along the sidewalk toward home. Everyone he saw was an imaginary policeman and they knew exactly what he carried in his jacket pocket. It would be an automatic trip to jail if he got caught. He picked up his pace and limped noticeably down the street. When he arrived at home, Jenny was nervously pacing the living room floor.

"Where have you been? I have been worried sick about you. Felix said you left work hours ago. Why didn't you call?" asked a concerned Jenny as she tried to make eye contact with her husband.

"Sorry, my cell phone is dead. I just went for a walk," he answered and went straight to the bathroom and locked the door. He removed the item from his jacket and stared at it for a few seconds, then looked at himself in the mirror and shook his head in disgust. He removed the lid from the toilet tank and carefully set the black velvet wrapped contraband inside, and replaced the lid. He washed his hands and face, and again stared at himself in the mirror. He felt himself unraveling. *This is not the same person who went forward to accept Christ as his Lord and Savior when he was a teenager,* he thought, and then slowly shook his head in disgust at what he had become.

Jenny knocked softly on the bathroom door. "Rob, are you okay?"

"Yeah, I just have a little stomach ache, that's all," he replied. "I'll be out in a minute."

Jenny returned to the kitchen and warmed Rob's dinner in the microwave oven. The baby kicked inside of her, temporarily taking her mind off the gut feeling she had that something was drastically wrong with Rob. It wasn't like him not to call when he was going to be late, especially with the baby due at any time.

Rob managed to approach Jenny from behind without her knowledge. He wrapped his arms around her big belly and kissed her softly on the nape of the neck, making her squirm. "Sorry, honey," he said. "I can barely get my arms around you anymore," he chuckled, changing the subject.

Jenny pulled away and turned to face him. "Rob, I feel like something is really wrong here. You seem to be falling apart and I'm really scared. You're missing work, staying out late, and this drinking—"

"Jen, I told you to stop worrying. I'm fine, okay? It's just this freakin' leg!"

"Maybe you should go back to the doctor?"

"Forget the doctors!" boomed Rob. "They don't give a rat's about me. All they'll say is that it's in my head again!"

"Rob, I know that God can heal you. Why don't we pray that—"

"Forget God too! He's the one that let all this happen!" yelled Rob as he stormed into the bedroom and slammed the door.

Jenny crumpled to the floor and began to cry. "God, please help us. Psalm 61 says, 'Hear my cry, O God; Attend to my prayer. From the end of the earth I will cry to You, when my heart is overwhelmed; Lead me to the rock that is higher than I.' That is my prayer, Lord. Please. Help us."

CHAPTER 13

The Fall

Early the next morning, Jenny was still asleep as Rob showered, shaved and dressed for work. He removed the black velvet wrapped contraband from the toilet tank and slipped it under his jacket. He went into the kitchen and took the keys to the Volkswagen from Jenny's purse and headed for the front door.

"Aren't you going to say goodbye?" she asked, standing in the bedroom doorway.

"Oh, you startled me. I thought you were sleeping."

Jenny noticed the car keys in his hand. "You're taking the car?"

"My leg has been really bothering me lately and those pills don't seem to be helping very much."

"Did you get your cell phone?" she asked. "I charged the battery for you last night."

Rob returned to the kitchen, unplugged the cell phone and stuck it in his jacket pocket. "Thanks, honey."

Jenny walked over to him and gave him a kiss on the lips. "I love you," she said. "Be careful."

Rob nodded and opened the front door. "Love you, too," he said softly. "And, don't worry. I haven't forgotten how to drive."

Rob left the apartment and limped hurriedly toward the parking lot. Aware of the objects under his coat he nervously looked around for anyone who looked like the police. He got into the car and immediately locked the door. Beads of perspiration formed on his upper lip and his mouth became dry. He removed the items from under his coat and put it in the glove compartment and slammed it shut. The parking lot was empty except for an alley cat headed for the dumpster. Rob started up the car and drove toward work. He was careful not to break any traffic laws because he did not want to get stopped by the police. The swollen, scarred leg throbbed and shooting pains shot up and down Rob's whole leg as he pulled into the deserted alley behind B & B Electronics. Beads of sweat permeated his forehead and his hands began to shake. "What the hell," he murmured under his breath as he reached to open the glove compartment. He stared for a moment at the black velvet cloth, struggling with the idea of using Lenny's painkiller. He shook his head as though losing a battle with himself, reached in, and removed it from the glove compartment. He looked in the rear view mirror and up and down the desolate alley. Nothing stirred. He could hear himself breathing, which was interrupted by a painful groan that seemed to emanate from deep down in his gut. Following Lenny's instructions, Rob prepared the syringe. His once muscular forearm showed some deep purple veins. *No problem finding a vein*, he thought as he pressed the needle against the fattest one. Rob plunged the needle into his arm and almost immediately his eyes rolled back in his head. He gently swayed from side to side, softly moaning. He felt no pain. He felt nothing. On the car seat next to him, Rob's cell phone rang several times, but he was unable to answer it, and he did not care.

—

Jenny paced nervously across the kitchen floor, a white cordless phone pressed to her ear. She suddenly clutched her stomach and bent over as a sharp pain enveloped her abdomen, and she dropped the telephone. "Rob, Rob... where are you?" she softly pleaded. Jenny picked up the phone and dialed Felix Werner's number.

"Hello?"

"Mr. Werner, the baby. I think the baby's coming!"

"Oh, oh my. Uh, where's Rob? Is he home?"

"I tried calling him on his cell phone, but he didn't answer. Oh!"

"I'll be right there. Don't move!"

Felix nervously slammed the telephone down on the receiver and frantically searched for his car keys. "Ha! There you are," he exclaimed as he found them in his pants pocket.

He arrived at Jenny's apartment and pounded on the door. "Jenny? Jenny!"

The door swung open and Felix was greeted by a bent over Jenny, holding her stomach with one hand and a small red suitcase in the other. "I think we better hurry!"

Felix reached out and took her suitcase, then grabbed her by the arm. "Come on, come on. Let's go. Oh, my," he said nervously as Jenny groaned.

The old Edsel skidded around the corner, nearly sideswiping a police car parked in a red zone in front of a fire hydrant. "He should get a ticket," yelled Felix. "Parking in front of a fire hydrant!"

Once at the hospital, the nurses took Jenny away from Felix and rushed her into the delivery room, leaving Felix holding her little red suitcase. A painful, worried look came across Felix's face. "Oh, Jenny, Jenny," he murmured as tears welled up in his eyes.

In the delivery room, the doctor and two nurses prepared for the birth. It seemed like every other minute Jenny writhed in pain. Minutes turned into hours, and finally Jenny gave birth to a beautiful, healthy baby boy.

After what seemed like an eternity to Felix, a nurse with long red hair entered the waiting room. "Congratulations. You have a new grandson."

"Grandson?" said Felix proudly. "Yes, a grandson," chuckling to himself.

"You can come with me," said the nurse, motioning the direction with her hand.

Felix followed her, exhibiting a newfound spring in his step. He smiled broadly, showing a tea stained, uneven collection of teeth as he entered Jenny's hospital room.

Jenny looked like she had been through the ringer. Her hair appeared as though it was combed with a garden rake and she was extremely pale. She gazed lovingly at the newborn baby boy cradled in her arm.

"She had a pretty rough time of it, so she needs some rest," advised the nurse, making sure Felix made eye contact with her.

"Oh, okay. I won't be long," he replied as he brushed past the nurse and came alongside Jenny's bed. "He is so beautiful, Jenny. He is the best looking baby in the whole hospital. A gift from God."

Felix took his eyes off of the baby and looked at Jenny. Tears flowed down her cheeks and she forced a slight smile.

"I'm sorry Rob isn't here to—"

"I know he would be here if he could," she interrupted.

"I will try to get a hold of him. Don't worry; I'll find him. You just get some rest."

The old man tenderly wiped a tear from Jenny's cheek, and then cradled the tiny baby's head in his hand. "They think that I'm your his Papa," he said with a grin. "I will find your daddy, don't worry," he added as he backed out of the room.

Felix went to a payphone in the hospital lobby and pulled out a handful of change. He placed a call to Rob's cell phone, but there was still no answer. *Maybe he was in an accident*, Felix thought as the furrows in his brow grew deeper.

Out in the hospital parking lot, Felix fired up the old Ford. "I'll drive around until I find him," he muttered. He drove up and down the streets looking in alleys and doorways. He stopped in front of a small, tough neighborhood bar and sat there for a minute or two in order to get up the courage to go inside. As he entered through the front door, several gruff looking patrons sized him up, which made Felix uneasy. When his eyes adjusted to the dark, he looked around for Rob, but he was nowhere to be found. Felix continued driving around the worst areas in town looking for Rob. The old man began to worry, which turned into stress. "Where are you, Rob?" he said aloud.

CHAPTER 14

Spiraling

Early the next morning, the sun poured through the Venetian blinds and onto the Jenny's hospital bed. It was a beautiful day, complete with a bright blue sky and puffy white clouds. The nurse carried Jenny's baby boy into the room and gently placed him in bed next to her. "What a beautiful little boy you have there, Mrs. Jacobs. Perfect, just perfect."

"Thank you. He is beautiful, isn't he?" replied Jenny as the phone rang, interrupting the moment.

"Hello, Mrs. Jacob's room," stated the nurse into the receiver.

"Hi, this is her husband, Mr. Jacobs. Is she all right?"

"Well, just where have you been, Mr. Jacobs?" sarcastically queried the nurse as Jenny reached for the telephone. Jenny took the telephone from the nurse and pressed it to her ear. "Rob?"

"Honey, I'm so, so sorry I wasn't there for you. Our neighbor said that Felix took you to the hospital. You and the baby are okay, right? I—"

"Where have you been?! How could you miss our son's birth? I thought something happened to you!"

"Don't be mad, Jen. I was, uh, helping this guy, and, uh—"

"I can't believe you. Where are your priorities?" she asked as her eyes welled up with tears.

"Look, I said I'm sorry. I'm coming down to the hospital right now, ok?"

"You'd better call Felix first."

Rob wrestled with the idea that he had to call Felix. On one hand, he knew it was the right thing to do, but on the other hand, he did not want to lie to him. He couldn't tell Felix the truth. Felix would just lose respect for him, and could not understand what he was going through. Rob tried to rationalize not calling, but he decided he didn't really have a choice.

Felix was busy stocking the shelves behind the counter when the telephone rang, breaking the silence in the empty store.

"Good morning! B & B Electronics." "Mr. Werner... Rob. I—"

"Rob, are you all right? We've been worried about you. Nobody knew where you were."

"Yes, I am sorry about that. I just want to thank you for taking Jenny to the hospital and all."

"Rob, are you sure everything is okay?" asked Felix sensing that there was something wrong.

"Yes, Mr. Werner, everything's fine. I'm heading over to the hospital right now, and I, uh, I won't be in today."

"That's fine, Rob, don't worry about it. But you know, you have missed quite a few days this month—"

"Yeah, I know... haven't been feelin' too good lately. I'll make it up to you. Well, I'd better get goin'," he said as he hung up the phone.

Rob walked into the bathroom and examined the needle mark on the inside of his left forearm. He ran his finger across the puncture wound and shook his head. He glanced at himself in the mirror, rolled down the sleeve, and buttoned his shirt. He left the apartment and rushed to the hospital.

Rob stood next to Jenny's hospital bed, held his newborn son in his arms, and lovingly gazed into the baby's eyes. Jenny smiled, "Well... I guess I forgive you. How can I stay mad at the man who gave me this beautiful boy?"

"I can't believe it. He's just so... so perfect," gushed Rob.

"Felix said our baby is a gift from God."

"Yeah. A gift," he whispered as his eyes welled up with tears. "Here, honey, you take him. Sometimes, I just don't feel worthy of you and... this baby."

"Don't be silly, Rob. We love you. Hey, let's name him after your father, Michael. Michael Robert Jacobs. Yeah, that sounds—"

"Just Michael, forget the Robert part," he mumbled, looking down at the floor.

"Rob, don't be so down on yourself."

"Look, I have to go to work. I'll be back tonight."

Rob leaned over and softly kissed Jenny on the cheek, turned and slowly walked out of the room.

"Bye, I love you," she shouted as he disappeared down the hallway.

—

Lenny's friend, Icabod, pushed the wheelchair down the dirty sidewalk and stopped in front of Lenny's apartment. The two stopped briefly to watch several cars and pedestrians go by.

Icabod Briscoe was known in the old neighborhood as the consummate petty thief. Anything that wasn't nailed down could vanish when he was around. He was basically homeless, until Lenny took him in, but even with all the amenities of an apartment, he still rarely bathed and gave off the odor of rotten onions. Now, he was addicted to drugs and sold them for Lenny wherever and whenever he could.

"Hey, Lenny, what happened to your war buddy the other night?" asked Icabod.

"War buddy?"

"Yeah, you know, the guy with the limp. What's his name? You know?"

"Oh, you mean Rob? The jarhead dude."

"Yeah, that's the guy. What's the story?"

"Guarantee he'll be back. I gave 'im a little free taste. Next time, gonna cost em though. Ha!"

In the crowded hospital parking lot, Rob fumbled for his car keys. He opened the car door and slid in behind the steering wheel, staring through the windshield as though in a trance. After a couple of minutes, he reached into his pants pocket and pulled out his cell phone and began frantically dialing a number. He pressed the cell phone hard up against his ear so as not to miss a word. The ring was answered immediately.

"Yeah, Lenny, here."

"Hey, Lenny. What's up, man? It's Rob."

"Rob! My man! We were just talkin' about you. I thought you'd be calling, but not this soon."

"I need to see you, like right away."

"Sure, come on over, we'll have a little party. Okay?"

"I'll be right there," said Rob nervously. He started up the car and tossed his cell phone on the passenger seat.

He drove at a high rate of speed for several miles until he spotted a black and white police car in his rear view mirror. His heart began to beat faster and harder, and he began to sweat. The black and white roared past him and disappeared in the distance. Rob glanced at the glove box a couple of times. *If the cops found my stash, I would go to jail for sure*, he thought. Rob pulled to the curb in front of the apartment building. He looked around to make sure there were no police, and then removed the black velvet bag from the glove compartment. Once at Lenny's apartment, he knocked softly, almost as if not wanting to disturb the occupants.

The door opened a few inches and Lenny's right hand man, Icabod, peered out.

"Hey, you're Rob, right? I'm Icky. How's it goin'? Come on in."

As the door swung open Rob heard Lenny yell, "Rob! Come on in, man. We been waitin' for you."

Rob stepped into the apartment and saw Lenny wheel himself out of the kitchen and over to the living room coffee table where there were several small bindles of heroine, some syringes, a couple spoons and a burning candle.

Lenny looked Rob up and down, and noticed Rob was holding the black velvet bag. "I see you brought your own kit," he chuckled.

"Yeah, the one you gave me," replied Rob as he gently dropped it on the coffee table.

"Ready to PARTY? Heh, heh," laughed Icky rather sinisterly.

"Not so fast, gentlemen," Lenny interjected. "I can't afford to give all my little goodies away. Rob, you got some dough on you?"

"Uh, I got a little bit. I—" Rob reached into his pocket and pulled out several bills. "Forty bucks. I got forty bucks."

"Dude, you need at least a hundred. This is good stuff… from China."

"Well all I got is forty."

"Okay, man, I'll spot you sixty bucks, but next time you better bring a hundred."

All three reached for the items on the coffee table at the same time.

"Whoa, Icky, slow down," warned Lenny. "Where's your manners? Guests first. Go ahead, Rob."

CHAPTER 15

Second Chance

Jenny finished packing the little red suitcase and sat quietly on the side of the hospital bed, staring out through the open door when a nurse suddenly appeared carrying the baby. "Hi, Mrs. Jacobs. Look who's here to see you, all ready to go home."

Jenny smiled and took the baby from the nurse. "My little angel."

"Isn't your husband coming to pick you up?" inquired the nurse.

Jenny shrugged her shoulders, "He was supposed to be here, but... I guess I could call Felix." She handed the baby back to the nurse and picked up the telephone on the nightstand. Felix answered on the first ring and was more than willing to come to Jenny's aid, even if he had to close the store to do it.

The Edsel hummed down the boulevard toward Jenny's apartment building. The old man gripped the steering with two hands as though he were wrestling a bull by the horns, a scowl on his face.

"You know, I had to close the store today in order to pick you up. Rob hasn't been showing up at work and if he keeps this up, I hate to say, I will have to let him go."

"I understand. I don't know what's going on with him lately. He's acting so strange. I'm so sorry, Mr. Werner."

"Felix. Call me Felix."

"I'm sorry… Felix."

Rob was passed out on the living room sofa. He had not shaved or bathed in days. His clothes were wrinkled and food stained. Three days worth of dishes were piled up in the sink and the smell of rotting leftovers rose from the kitchen trashcan.

Felix and Jenny arrived at the apartment. She carried the bundled up baby tightly in her arms, followed by Felix, who carried the little red suitcase and a bouquet of red roses. Jenny unlocked the door and they entered the apartment. They both spotted Rob about the same time.

"Well, there's Rob. He's out like a light," said Felix.

"Thank you, Felix, for everything. Let me put the baby down and I'll get Rob—"

"No, no. Don't wake him. I've got to get back," he advised. "When he wakes up, tell him I'd like to speak with him down at the store."

Felix set the little suitcase down, put the flowers on the coffee table and backed out toward the front door. He nodded at Jenny, who nodded back and he closed the door behind him.

Jenny carried the tiny baby into the bedroom and laid him in the bassinet. The baby immediately began to cry and Jenny tried to comfort him. However, the baby's cry grew louder and he showed the power of his lungs. On the sofa, Rob began to squirm. He sat up, disoriented for a moment, and then realized it was a child's cry. *A baby? That's… MY baby,* he thought, placing a hand on his throbbing forehead. "Jenny!" he yelled with anticipation.

Jenny came into the room holding the whimpering baby, who stopped crying shortly after being picked up by his mother. "Rob, what's wrong with you? What's going on?"

"What?" he replied trying to shake the cobwebs from his head. "I'm sick, I just don't feel well. I—"

"You're going to lose your job," she interrupted. "How long do you think Felix is going to put up with this?"

"I'm sick and tired of that old man. He's always meddling in our business."

"That old man has been a Godsend. It's YOU, Rob. YOU are the problem."

"Fine. You want me to leave? I will."

"No, that's not what I said. The baby and I NEED you. We need you to be responsible and take care of us," pleaded Jenny as she reached out and grabbed Rob by the arm. "Rob, I love you. What's wrong with you?"

Rob pulled away from her grasp, "I have to go out for a while."

"Go out?! Felix wants to speak with you down at the store."

"Fine. I'll be back later," he said as he grabbed his jacket and walked out the door.

When the door closed behind him, Jenny burst out in tears. "Oh God... I don't know what to do."

It was almost closing time at the B & B Electronics Store. Felix was finishing up with a lone customer when Rob entered the store. He pretended to browse the isles until the customer left, and then approached Felix who was standing behind the counter.

"Rob, what's wrong? You have been acting very strange lately. You've missed work, and... look at you, you—"

"I'm sick, Felix."

"Sick? You look like hell. When's the last time you took a shower?"

"Look, I'm sorry. I—"

"Rob, I gave you a job here. I tried to help you and Jenny. Now, you got a baby. If you don't pull yourself together... I'm gonna have to let you go," warned Felix.

"Felix, please... I need this job."

"Well, I need someone here that I can count on."

"Just give me another chance, I promise I won't let you down."

"Well... okay. Just this one last chance, Rob. Now, go home and get yourself cleaned up."

"Thanks, Felix."

Felix followed Rob out the front door and onto the sidewalk. Rob got into his car and drove off down the road. Felix stood there and watched with a furrowed brow until Rob's car disappeared in the distance. He slowly shook his head and shuffled back into the store.

Rob drove erratically as he reached for the cell phone on the passenger seat. He finally snatched it up and slowly dialed a number. It rang several times before being answered.

"Lenny! This is Rob. I got to see you."

"I'm a little busy right now. Call me later," advised Lenny.

"I really need to see you *now*," begged Rob.

"Look, Rob, the price has gone up. From now on, it's a hundred bucks a pop."

"A hundred? How am I gonna get that kind of money?"

"That don't concern me, dude. That's the going rate. Take it or leave it."

"Okay, okay. I'll be at your place around 9:30 tonight."

"See ya."

CHAPTER 16

Missing in Action

Felix paced back and forth behind the long counter at the B & B Electronics Store. He stopped occasionally to check the large round clock on the wall. "10," he said as a matter-of-fact. *Rob is already an hour late for work*, he thought.

Another hour passed and Felix stared at the clock. "Still no Rob," he whispered as he picked up the phone and called Rob's apartment.

"Hello," answered Jenny.

"Felix," he announced. "Is Rob there?"

"No, he left for work hours ago."

"Never showed up, Jenny. I'm sorry to say this, but I'm going to have to let him go. I've given him so many chances. I'm sorry."

"I understand, Felix," she said painfully and hung up the phone.

Tears welled up in her eyes as she picked the phone back up and angrily dialed Rob's cell phone. It rang several times and went to voice mail. Jenny tearfully left a message, "Rob, Felix just called and said he was letting you go. You didn't show up for work this morning. What's going on? Did you find someone else? Please call me."

Two hours later, Rob slid into the driver's seat of his car. He glanced over at his cell phone on the passenger seat and noticed he had missed a call. After listening to Jenny's message, he sheepishly called her. She answered the phone on the first ring, but there was silence on the other side. "Rob, is that you? Rob?"

Finally, after what seemed like an eternity to Jenny, Rob answered, "I'm sorry, honey. I let Felix down, I let you and the baby down. I really want to do better, Jenny, I just… I don't know—"

"Just come home, Rob," she said and hung up the telephone.

But Rob had other plans.

CHAPTER 17

The Betrayal

Rob slowly drove down the dark deserted alley behind the electronics store, turned off the headlights and coasted to a stop behind Felix's old blue Edsel. Rob looked at his watch, *five minutes till closing time*, he thought. Beads of perspiration formed on his upper lip and brow. He gripped the steering wheel tightly with both hands and shook his head as though trying to ward off a demon. He started the engine, put the car in drive and lifted his foot off the brake, but then suddenly stopped. "9:00 p.m., closing time," he mumbled as he looked at the clock on the dashboard. He then turned off the engine and tried to light a cigarette, but his hands shook so much that he gave up on it and tossed the cancer stick out the car window. Frustrated, he leaned over, opened the glove compartment, and pulled out a military .45 caliber automatic. He removed the clip, examined it, and then slammed it back into the gun. He stared at the gun for a minute, and then he slid it into his waistband.

Felix exited the rear of the electronics store and looked up and down the quiet alley. As usual, nothing moved. He locked the door with the keys he held in his left hand. In his right hand, he held a cloth bank bag that contained the week's receipts.

Rob slipped on the black ski mask as he watched as the old man walk toward his car unaware of any danger. Felix looked up and was suddenly face to face with the masked man.

"Hand it over!"

"What?" said a startled Felix.

Rob pulled the gun from his waistband and shoved it into the old man's face. "Now! Give me the money!" he demanded as he reached out and pulled the bank bag out of Felix's hand.

Felix stared into the eyes of the masked bandit. "I know who you are. I know you."

Rob turned, ran back to his car and started the engine. The car roared out of the alley as Felix stood motionless and watched as a cloud of bluish exhaust dissipated in the darkness.

—

The smell from the trash in Lenny's kitchen permeated the tiny apartment. In a haze of cigarette smoke, Lenny, Icky and Rob sat around the coffee table in a drug-induced stupor. They were all under the influence of black tar heroin.

Lenny leaned back in his wheelchair, looked at his two cohorts and began to chuckle. "You guys are really high. It must be some good stuff," he giggled. "Rob, you gotta come up with some more money, dude. Like, you owe me big time."

"Don't go bummin' me out, man. Besides, I never seen Icky pay you?"

"Wait a minute, dude. Icky's my top salesman. He don't get no free ride," growled Lenny. "You need to get with the program."

"I can't sell the stuff, Lenny. I got a family."

"Look, Jarhead, you owe me over a grand and you better pay me now!"

"I told you, I ain't got it."

"Like I said, you gotta get with the program."

"Okay, okay," relinquished Rob as he laid his head back on the sofa.

CHAPTER 18

Evicted

Jenny stared out her living room window as she held her baby close to her bosom. The rocking chair glided back and forth in a rhythmic manor as the baby fell fast asleep. At Jenny's feet was an Eviction Notice from the landlord. She got up from the chair and set the baby down on the couch. *I need to call my mother*, she thought as she picked up the telephone and dialed her number.

"Hello?" her mother answered.

"Hi, Mom. What you doing?"

"Just sitting here with your stepfather, planning our next cruise, you know?" she replied sensing something wrong in Jenny's voice. "Is everything all right? Is the baby okay?"

"We're fine, Mom. It's… Rob. He hasn't worked in months. He disappears for days on end, and he's not taking care of himself."

"Is it his leg?"

"I think that's only part of it and that's what started it. I think he's on drugs," said Jenny as she started to cry.

"Oh, no, I can't believe that," replied her mother. "I was afraid he might get addicted to those darn pain pills," she added.

"Mom, I just got an eviction notice. The landlord wants us out before the first of next month. I don't know what I'm going to do," cried Jenny.

"Honey, it's going to be okay. You got to trust the Lord. Remember, all things work out for good for those who love Him."

"Can the baby and I move back home with you for a while? At least until I can find a job and a place of my own?"

"Of course, dear."

"Don't you have to talk it over with Dad?"

"Did you forget who is the boss in this family?" she chuckled. "Besides, you know Daddy won't hesitate to help his baby girl."

"Thanks, Mom. I love you."

Jenny immediately went into the bedroom and removed two large suitcases from the closet. She hurriedly packed all of her clothes in the suitcases, and stuffed the baby's clothes and some toys in a large plastic trash bag.

Jenny was startled when the telephone rang shattering the quiet apartment. She ran to answer the phone. "Rob?" she asked worriedly.

"Oh, hello Jenny, this is Felix. I haven't heard from you in a while. I thought I'd call and see how you are doing. How are you and the baby?"

Jenny begins to cry. "We just got evicted, but Michael and I are going to stay with my parents until I find a job."

"I'm sorry to hear that. Have you heard from Rob?" "He came by last week and left some grocery money. He looks awful. Lost about 25 pounds."

"He needs help. I think he has a drug problem."

"It's something. I just don't know what to do."

"Maybe, something like AA? I'm not sure? Is there anything I can do for you and the baby?"

"Thanks, Felix, but we'll be okay."

"Don't hesitate to call me. God bless."

Jenny continued to pack up her belongings and opened one of Rob's dresser drawers. Under some of his clothes, she found his .45 caliber auto. It stunned her for a moment, and then she picked it up and held it in her hand. She was somewhat surprised by how heavy the gun was. She studied it for a moment, turned and tossed it onto the bed. Rifling through the rest of the clothes, Jenny found a piece of paper with an address scribbled on it in Rob's handwriting. She couldn't make out all of the numbers, but she recognized the street. *Forty three hundred block of Main Street*, she thought. *What or who is over there?*

CHAPTER 19

Busted

Rob stood next to the pay phone outside the corner liquor store at 42nd Street and Main Street. He fearfully looked up and down the street for police cars, but spotted Icky moving toward him on the sidewalk like a nervous racehorse. "Hey, Rob, doin' any good? How's business?"

"It could be better," quipped Rob.

"What you got left?"

"Just one bag. Why?"

"You could give it to me," chuckled Icky.

"I got to sell this puppy, man. You know, Lenny keeps bugging me for money."

"Okay, be that way. See ya at Lenny's later, right?"

"Yeah, right."

A black and white patrol car pulled around the corner from Rob and Icky. Impulsively, they turned away from each other and began walking in opposite directions. The officers exited their vehicle and walked briskly after Rob. "Hold it! Hold it right there!" yelled the big, muscular cop holding a black nightstick in his left hand. His other hand rested on the handle of his holstered police revolver.

Icky continued to walk away, but never looked back or acknowledged the police officers. Rob froze in his tracks, as Icky disappeared around the corner.

The shorter of the two officers menacingly approached Rob with his hand on his gun butt, "Keep your hands where I can see 'em, buddy," he commanded.

The big officer reached out and grabbed Rob by the arm, spun him around and pushed him up against the liquor store's brick wall. "You ain't got any guns, knives, or hand grenades on you, do you?" quipped the officer as he patted Rob down.

"Hand grenades? What?" said a confused Rob.

"Hey. Just kiddin. He's clean, partner. No weapons."

The shorter officer approached Rob. "I don't think I've seen you around here before. You got some ID? Driver's license?"

"Yes, sir. I do," answered Rob as he nervously reached into his pocket and pulled out his wallet, which was bulging with cash. "I think I've got my license here, somewhere."

"Right there, Buddy," said the shorter cop, pointing to it in Rob's wallet. "Not from around here, are you?" he added suspiciously.

"Oh, here? No, I don't live around here."

"You work in this area?"

"No, sir. I'm outta work right now," Rob replied.

"You got quite a large amount of cash for someone who's unemployed. Step over here, and empty your pockets on the hood of my police car."

"Is this necessary, officers? I was just on my way home."

The big muscular police officer tapped the hood of the police car with his nightstick. "Right here! Everything. On the car."

Rob put his wallet, a set of car keys, some loose change, a handkerchief and a small pocketknife on the hood of the car.

"Is that it?" asked the big officer.

"Yes, sir," replied Rob as he tried to read the officer's nameplate. "Officer... Murphy."

"Now, turn your pockets inside out."

Rob turned out his front pockets and a small bindle of heroin fell to the sidewalk.

"Well, well, well, look what we have here," declared officer Murphy.

Rob looked down at his feet and shook his head. "That's not mine. I don't now where that came from."

"Did it fall from the sky, Chicken Little? It FELL out of YOUR pocket, stupid!"

"Okay, buddy. Take off your jacket and roll up your sleeves," ordered Murphy.

Rob removed his jacket and partially rolled up the sleeves on his plaid shirt. Officer Murphy pushed Rob's left sleeve up higher to reveal a series of needle tracks.

"Well, what do we have here? Got more tracks than the Southern Pacific," quipped Murphy.

"No, sir. That's just where I fell into the rose bushes," advised Rob.

Both the officers began laughing out loud. "Rose bushes! That's the first time I heard that one. Sure your cat didn't scratch you?" laughed Murphy. "James, hook 'em up."

Officer James handcuffed Rob and placed him in the back seat of the police car. Both Officer James and Murphy continued to laugh as they drove off toward the police station. In the darkness, Icky watched intently until the black and white disappeared from view and then made his way to Lenny's apartment.

Lenny sat quietly in his wheelchair while Icky paced nervously back and forth across the living room floor. "What are we gonna do? They busted Rob. We ought to get outta here," mumbled Icky as he continued to pace the floor.

"Will you SIT DOWN. You're making me nervous. Look, Icky, Rob ain't gonna give us up. He's the loyal type, you know… Semper Fi, always faithful."

"Yeah, that's right. Well, what if the cops are on to us?" whined Icky.

"They would have been all over us by now if they knew anything. Don't worry about it."

"What about Rob?" asked Icky.

"We're gonna bail him out. I'm gonna give you some money and you're going down to Puglisi's Bail Bonds. They'll take care of the rest."

"You'd do the same for me, right Lenny?"

"Yeah, right."

In a cold, dank cell in the city jail, Rob sat on the edge of his bunk. His stomach ached and he had to go to the bathroom, but the toilet in his cell was already overflowing. The stench of stale urine filled his nostrils and made him nauseous. Rob's head rested in both hands as he mumbled incoherently. The jailer noisily made his way back to Rob's cell, his keys gangling. "Jacobs!"

Rob jumped to his feet. "Did you say, Jacobs?"

"You're the only Jacobs here, aren't you?" said the jailer, unlocking Rob's cell. "Let's go!"

"Go? Go where?"

"What do you think, genius? You've been bailed out. Somebody up there likes you," he said, and rolled his eyes toward the ceiling.

The jailer led Rob to the release desk where he was given back his personal property. He put on his watch, placed his keys and wallet in his pocket, and last, he slowly slid on his wedding ring with a lingering look.

Officer James approached Rob just as he was about to be released. "Listen PUNK. I'll see you in court. Just 'cause your mommy bailed you out doesn't mean you're FREE. Best be watchin' your back."

Rob dropped his head and was shown to the exit door by one of the jailers. He felt that he'd reached the lowest point of his life. *I'd be better off dead*, he thought.

CHAPTER 20

Deep Slide

Lucy's Coffee Shop was affectionately called the Roach Café by the locals who frequented the small neighborhood-eating establishment. The smell of burnt coffee and bacon seemed to always permeate the air, and an occasional cockroach was seen scurrying across the floor. Greasy Joe, the cook, and Fat Flo, the waitress, were the sole employees on the premises. Rob and Icky, the only customers, sat huddled whispering in a back booth when Lenny wheeled his wheelchair up to their table.

"Rob, Rob, Rob," chimed Lenny, shaking his head. "You are just getting deeper and deeper into my wallet."

"Lenny, I swear I am gonna pay you back, every last dime. I swear it."

"Damn right! With interest, Jarhead," barked Lenny.

"Yeah… interest," chuckled Icky.

"Shut up, Icky!" said Rob angrily.

"Seems like you're into me for a few grand, Rob. Maybe even more, since I had to bail you out and the cops kept all the money and stuff as evidence," lectured Lenny. "Tell you what, you wanna pay back a small portion of what you owe me? I got a little job for you."

"Job? What kind of job?"

"I need you to pick up a package for me. Think you can do that?" asked Lenny.

"Sure, I can do that. Is that it?" asked Rob. Lenny nodded.

At midnight, Rob walked down a dark, desolate alley in a light drizzle. He pulled the black sweatshirt's hood up over his head and thrust his hands into his pockets as he slowly moved down the alley. A black cat suddenly jumped out from behind some trashcans and startled Rob. He stopped at the back of a warehouse that had the name "Blaine Imports" painted on the door. He looked up and down the alley, and then knocked softly on the door, but there was no response. After a few seconds, he knocked even louder, and then waited. The door slowly opened and a large man, about 60 years old, dressed all in black with a mustache and goatee stuck his head out and looked up and down the alley.

"You haven't been followed have you?" asked the stranger.

"Followed? Uh... no, I don't think so," answered Rob as he looked up and down the alley.

"Hurry! Get in here."

Rob jumped through the open doorway and the door slammed behind him.

"I'm here for the... package," whispered Rob nervously.

"I don't think I have met you before. I am Phillipe, and you are?"

"Rob, Rob Jacobs."

"Yes, Lenny told me all about you. Marine. Desert Storm hero, and all that."

"I'm no hero."

"I need to see your identification. I have to be sure who I am dealing with. You understand, Rob, don't you?"

"Here's my driver's license."

"No, that could be fake. Roll up your right pant leg."

Rob was puzzled by the request, but complied with Phillipe's request and showed a deformed, scarred right leg.

"That's good enough for me. Lenny said you got a Purple Heart for that. Follow me," said the Frenchman.

Phillipe led Rob through a maze of boxes and crates until he came to a small box with red lettering from Hong Kong. Phillipe handed it to Rob.

"Hong Kong, huh?" queried Rob.

"The less you know the better. Remember, we have never met. Give my regards to Lenny."

Phillipe showed Rob out the back door, and the door slammed loudly behind him. Rob looked up and down the alley. It was raining now and he stashed the small wooden box under his shirt and began to walk down the alley in the direction from which he came.

He was almost out of the alley when he heard a noise behind him. He turned and saw a black and white police car coming toward him. He picked up his pace and almost made it to the street when his path was suddenly blocked by another police car. He had no place to go. He froze, completely soaked with the wooden box still under his shirt. Two uniformed police officers exited their vehicle and approached Rob.

"Well, well, well. Look who we have here," quipped Officer James.

"What you carrying under your shirt, buddy?" asked Officer Murphy.

Rob took the small wooden box out from under his shirt. "This? I found this in the alley. I… I don't know what's in it."

"Yeah, right. Santa Claus left it for you," said Officer Murphy sarcastically with a grin.

"No, it's not mine. I mean… I found it in the alley."

"Drop the box, turn around and put your hands on your head," ordered Officer James.

Rob dropped the box in a puddle of rainwater and it broke open on one side. He stood straight as though at attention and put his hands on his head as ordered. Officer James approached him and immediately handcuffed him while Officer Murphy picked up the box and examined in closely. "Looky here, James, China White. Looks like we got ourselves a major heroin dealer."

"Let's go, punk," ordered Officer James as he grabbed Rob by the arm and led him to the police car. "You got the right to remain silent, you have the right to an attorney, and—"

Rob found himself back in the same jailhouse, only now the charges were a lot more serious. The gray haired old jailer finished fingerprinting him and stated as a matter of fact, "You got one phone call, Jacobs."

"I got nobody to call, officer."

"I thought you had a wife and kid?" asked the jailer.

"They'd be better off without me," replied Rob softly.

"Yep, probably would," snickered the jailer as he took Rob by the arm and led him to a jail cell.

—

The courthouse seemed unusually slow for a Monday morning. Rob was to be arraigned on two felony counts of possession of heroin for sale. He was escorted into the courtroom and was seated in the jury box along with several other prisoners. Rob glanced nervously around the courtroom and saw Jenny and Felix sitting in the front row. He smiled briefly and then a wave of embarrassment swept over him.

"You Jacobs?" asked a short, fat, balding man in a wrinkled double-breasted, pinstriped suit. "I'm Lou Stein, Public Defender. I've been assigned to be your attorney."

Stein had a reputation of being a stickler for detail. He also held the record for being in contempt of court and served time in county lock up on several occasions. Rob looked up at the man in front of him and nodded, then hung his head.

"We're first on the arraignment list this morning," stated Stein. "Hope the judge is in a good mood today," he added. "When they call your name, come over here and stand next to me. I'll do all the talking, okay?"

A few minutes passed, when the bailiff announced the arrival of Judge Heinz, a 60-year-old devout Jew with a short white goatee, black-rimmed glasses, wearing a black robe. The judge had the reputation of being a by the book, hard-nosed, sarcastic, no-nonsense member of the judiciary. He took his position behind the bench. "I see we have Deputy District Attorney Lee Perlman, for the people this morning," chimed the Judge. "And, Mr. Stein, for the defense. You actually made it on time today, Mr. Stein. Congratulations," he added sarcastically.

"Good morning, your honor," Stein sheepishly replied.

"Enough of the informalities, let's get along with it," grumbled Judge Heinz. "Let's see, first up— Jacobs. Robert Jacobs," he read out loud.

Rob stood next to Mr. Stein, and glanced over his shoulder at Jenny who nervously wrung her hands in distress.

"For the record, Public Defender Lou Stein, representing the defendant," announced Stein.

"Mr. Robert Jacobs, you are being arraigned this morning on two counts of possession of heroin for sale. Both felonies. You have been apprised of the charges against you. Has anyone tried to coerce you or make a deal with you in regard to a plea?" asked Judge Heinz.

"Excuse me, your honor," interrupted Deputy D.A. Perlman. "After speaking to Mr. Jacob's counsel, the prosecution has agreed to drop one of the counts in consideration to a guilty plea."

"Is that true, Mr. Stein?" asked the judge.

"Yes, your honor. I have conferred with my client and he wishes to make a plea."

"Mr. Jacobs, is that correct? You wish to plead guilty to one count of possession of heroin for sale, a felony? On your own free will?" asked Judge Heinz.

"Yeah, I guess so. I mean, yes, your honor," replied Rob.

"You understand, Mr. Jacobs, that by entering a guilty plea you give up your right to a trial, and you can be sentenced to spend a minimum of 18 months in the state prison?" asked the judge.

"Yes, I understand."

"Are you also aware that even with no prior convictions, you could get the maximum sentence of seven years? I could sentence you to seven years!"

"Yes, sir," answered Rob.

"How do you plead, Mr. Jacobs?" asked the judge.

"Guilty, your honor."

"Judge, sir. Before you hand down the sentence may I address the court?" asked Mr. Stein.

"You may, but make it quick," cautioned Judge Heinz.

"Your honor, my client, Mr. Jacobs, served honorably in the marines, sir, and is a disabled veteran of the Persian Gulf War. He has been awarded the Purple Heart and other medals of valor. Mr. Jacobs is married and is the father of a baby boy," stated Stein, glancing back at Jenny in the front row. "He is also an addict, your honor, due to the pain from the wounds he received in Iraq. He should be in a special rehabilitation program, your honor. I say all this in order for the court to consider leniency."

"Is that all, Mr. Stein?" asked the judge without waiting for an answer. "I have taken everything into consideration, and I hereby sentence you, Mr. Jacobs, to 3 years in state prison."

Rob turned and looked at Jenny and Felix. He forced a smile as he was led away by two sheriff's deputies, and mouthed the words, "I love you." Jenny watched him leave the courtroom in disbelief. She gripped Felix's coat sleeve tightly and burst into tears. "Oh, my God, Felix. I don't believe it. This is like a nightmare."

"Trust in the Lord, Jenny," he said as a matter of fact.

"I'm trying," Jenny whispered and Jeremiah 16:19 came to her mind: *O Lord, my strength and my fortress, my refuge in the day of affliction.*

CHAPTER 21

Prison Bound

The old silver bus headed down the one lane asphalt road toward the gray fortress that was surrounded by a double fence topped with razor wire. Guards armed with carbine rifles manned the ominous gun towers, vigilantly watching for any attempt at escape.

Rob looked out the bus window at snow-capped Mt. Baldy in the distance and then got his first glimpse of the prison. A feeling of nausea came over him, followed by a sharp pain in the gut. He doubled over and grabbed his stomach, holding back the urge to vomit.

After being herded off of the bus, the handcuffed and shackled inmates walked single-file into the main prison yard. Rob quickly surveyed his new environment.

"Hey, officer, bring that cute one over here," yelled an unseen inmate from inside one of the prison dorms. "Yeah," yelled another. "We like new fish!"

Rob pretended he did not hear the catcalls, but they made him fearful of what might come. "Let's go. Move it!" yelled one of the guards breaking Rob's train of thought. The guards led them to a large building where the new inmates were given a change of clothes and some bedding. He was then escorted to a cell by another guard who unlocked it and motioned for Rob to go inside. "Home sweet home," quipped the guard with a chuckle as he slammed the door shut behind Rob.

Rob immediately noticed that he had a roommate. He was a large, brawny black man about thirty years old with a shaved head. Rob sized him up quickly. "Hi. My name's Rob, Rob Jacobs," he announced as he extended his hand.

The new cellmate glanced at Rob's hand and turned away. "I don't know why they gotta put some white boy in here wit me? Dat jus' ain' right, man."

"Whadda you mean by that?" asked Rob.

"You ain' nevah been in da joint before, huh, crackah? They is prison rules, and they is prison rules."

Rob was still puzzled. "What?"

The cellmate shook is head. "If you is black, you don't hang with no whitie. If you La Raza, you chill wit you homeboys. And, if you white, you hang wit da othah crackahs. Ya get it?"

"Oh, yeah, I see. So, what if I hang out with some black guys?"

"You get yo'self killed. We gotta get you 'nother cell mate, boy."

Rob grabbed his stomach in pain. "Ugh… my stomach."

"Oh, no! You one of dem dope fiends, boy? Gonna have da fits, cold turkey? Nope, no, uh –uh, not in my pad. You gotta go, boy!"

Rob started to become nauseous and grabbed at his stomach again. "You know what? I ain't going anywhere," he mocked. "This is my PAD now too, alright?

"We'll see about that," taunted the big, muscular cellmate as he pushed Rob.

Rob pushed back, and sent his cellmate careening into the bunk beds. He bounced back and struck Rob with a left hook that decked him, causing a nosebleed.

"Get up! Get up!"

Rob jumped to his feet, lunged at his opponent, and tackled him. The two rolled around on the cell floor for a few minutes, each threw punches from various angles. Other inmates were now aware of the fight that was transpiring and began cheering. It was obvious the inmates had taken sides, black against white. An alarm pierced the air as several correctional officers dressed in riot gear and carrying nightsticks ran toward the cell. They were led by Sergeant Sharky, a 36-year-old, muscular ex-marine, who was feared by both his peers and the inmates. Sharky had the reputation of only asking you to comply one time, and if you didn't, he would let his baton do the talking.

"Open that cell!" Sergeant Sharky ordered one of the officers. The two continued to roll around the floor, throwing punches. "Break it up, you two!" Sharky then swung his baton and struck Rob on the back of the head. Rob rolled off to one side, groggy from the blow. His opponent jumped to his feet and stood at attention.

"Did you start this Richardson?" demanded Sergeant Sharky as Richardson remained silent at attention.

Rob got to his feet and rubbed the back of his head. Blood trickled from his nose onto his upper lip. "It looks like somebody just earned a stay in solitary. Who started it!" barked the Sergeant.

"I did. I started it," said Rob. Richardson glanced at Rob in amazement through swollen eyes. *Why did he take the blame?* thought Richardson.

"Take him," ordered Sharky, and his men grabbed Rob and led him from the cell as the other inmates cheered. "This doesn't look good for you Jacobs. Written up and put in the hole on your first day!"

CHAPTER 22

Solitary

Rob was curled up in a fetal position on the cold, dank floor of the solitary confinement cell. The silence was occasionally broken by his painful moans, as he shook uncontrollably. He had been like this for the past five days, battling the demons of heroin withdrawal. The food and water that had been placed in his cell went untouched for days.

On the sixth day, Rob sat up on the floor of his cell with his back to the cold cinder blocks. There was a week's growth of beard on his gaunt face, his eyes were sunken into his head, and he smelled as bad as he looked.

"Jacobs! Well, I see that you made it. You're still alive. Are you ready for some chow?" asked Sergeant Sharky.

"Uh, no sir," replied Rob weakly. "Just water... May I have some water, sir?"

"Water? Yeah, sure. You can have some water."

Sharky opened the cell door, entered and filled a paper cup with water from the sink and handed it to Rob. Rob's hand shook so much that he was unable to drink from the cup and he spilled most of it on his stained t-shirt. Sharky took the cup from Rob, refilled it and held it to Rob's lips as he drank.

"Thanks. Thank you, sir," said Rob.

"What branch of the military were you in Jacobs? Nobody in here ever calls me sir."

"Marines, sir. Persian Gulf."

"Viet Nam. Two tours. Now, I fight my battles in here," said Sharky. "You better listen up, marine. You got two more weeks in the hole. When you get out, best keep your nose clean. You got off on a bad foot, Jacobs."

"Yes, sir, I know."

"Your cellie has been concerned about you. Been askin' about you everyday."

"My cellie?"

"Yeah, you know, your sparring partner? Richardson, Ben Richardson," grinned Sharky as he slammed the cell door behind him.

Another week passed and Rob was feeling better since going cold turkey. He was now able to eat and drink. He still needed a bath and some fresh clothes. He heard the key turn in his cell's lock and the door opened. There stood two correctional officers. One carried a bundle of clean clothes. The other carried soap, a shaver, and a towel. "Let's go, Jacobs. Here, take this and come with us. You need a shower, man!"

The other correctional officer held his nose. "Whew, dude. You stink. Come on, let's go. This way." Rob was escorted down the hallway to the showers. As they passed by several cells, a black inmate yelled, "Hey, white boy, you dead meat! We 'eard wat you did to dat brotha. Bettah watch yo' back." Rob ignored the jeers and taunts.

After he shaved, showered and dressed in new prison blues, Rob was shown to his new cell. The first thing he noticed was that there was only one bunk. *No cellmate, good,* he thought. There was a toilet, a sink and some graffiti on the walls.

It was time for the evening meal, so several correctional officers escorted inmates single file from Rob's cellblock over to the mess hall. Rob grabbed a tray and got in the mess hall line. He approached the first server, a tall black inmate who was behind the counter wearing a white apron and a white cap. Rob held out his tray. The server took a ladle full of hot beans and poured it over Rob's hands. Even though it was very hot, Rob did not show any emotion or react in any way. Rob went to the next server, who was also black, and held out his tray. The server took a ladle of hot mashed potatoes and flopped it onto Rob's tray with such force that it splattered on his shirt. Again, Rob did not react and continued on to the next station where a white inmate gave him a ladle full of a gray substance with the consistency of oatmeal. "What's that?" asked Rob.

"Mystery Meat, dude."

Rob carried his tray and looked around the mess hall for a place to sit. The smell of the food almost caused him to lose his appetite. He heard the sound of several inmates participating in a belching contest. "Nice," he said sarcastically. A muscular white inmate, who was covered with tattoos, including a large swastika on his neck, approached him. "I'm Kurt. I heard about you kickin' that brotha's butt. Come on, you can sit with us," he said as he pointed in the direction with his chin. Rob followed Kurt to a dining hall table that was full of tattooed white supremacists. Before he sat down, he looked around the large dining hall. His eyes met the eyes of Ben Richardson, who was seated with a group of black prisoners. Ben shook his head in disapproval of Rob's chosen dinner companions as Rob sat down.

Across the table from Rob sat a 33-year-old inmate with more tattoos than clean white skin. He leered across the table at Rob. His wide grin, which was missing every other tooth, reminded Rob of a jack-o-lantern.

"You're quite the celebrity around here. This your first time in the joint?" he asked. Rob just nodded to the affirmative.

"Well, you better hang with us or you won't last too long in here," he added.

"Yeah, that's right," interjected Kurt. "We got each others back," he said as he looked across the dining hall to where the large group of black inmates sat, and then to the other end where a large group of Hispanic prisoners were seated.

"You're already a target, man," chuckled the Jack-o-Lantern faced inmate.

Rob looked around the huge mess hall as he ate his food, and noticed it was all divided by race. The group he was with was all white, Richardson was seated with all the blacks, and then there was a group of Hispanics. Then Rob noticed a small group of mixed races sitting to one side of the dining hall. "Who are those guys?" asked Rob.

"Those guys? Oh, they're what we call the weak ones. You know, the so-called Christians," answered Jack-o-Lantern. "They need a crutch."

Out on the prison exercise yard, Rob walked around the track by himself. He looked at the snow-capped mountains and marveled at a flock of ducks that were headed south, flying in a "V" formation. As he looked back down at the track he noticed Ben Richardson and another huge black inmate, almost seven feet tall, approaching.

"We needa talk," stated Ben.

"I don't need to talk to you," answered Rob curtly. "Who is this, your body guard?" Rob added.

"No seriously, man, we needa talk," said Ben sternly.

Rob started to walk away and Ben reached out and grabbed him by the arm. "Don't!" Rob yelled as he jerked away and braced himself for a fight.

Ben turned to the large black giant of a man, "Terrell, take off. I needa talk wid dis man, alone." Terrell nodded, turned and walked away.

"Say what you got to say, and make it quick," stated Rob.

"Lis'en. Thanks for takin' da blame for da fight," said Ben softly.

"Don't mention it."

"No, man, it took some guts ta take da heat. I respect you fo' dat."

"Yeah, fine," said Rob as he started to turn and walk away.

"Jacobs!" yelled Ben. I wouldn' be hangin' out wit all dem White Power dudes. Dey bad news, man," he added as he turned and walked in the direction opposite of Rob, while black and white inmates watched with curiosity from a distance.

CHAPTER 23

The Letter

Jenny grinned broadly and held her baby's hands as he attempted to take his first steps across his grandmother's living room carpet. "Come on, Sweetie," coaxed Grandma. "Come to Grandma," she laughed. Jenny let go of his hands and the baby took two awkward steps toward Grandma's outstretched hands. "He did it! He did it," bursted Grandma. "He took his first steps!" Grandma gathered him up in her arms and smothered him with kisses.

"My little man, walking already. Can you believe it?" chimed Jenny. "At nine months."

"I wish his father could have been here to see it," said Jenny's mother.

"I think I am going to go visit him soon," added Jenny as her eyes welled up with tears. She turned and quickly walked to the bathroom, leaving the baby with her mother.

—

Rob sat on the edge of his bunk and read Jenny's latest letter. His eyes teared up and he dabbed at them with the back of his forefinger.

Dear Rob,
I hope you are doing okay. I miss you so much. Michael took
his first steps today. Mom and I were so excited. He is growing

up too fast. I know that you would like to have been there, but you will be home before you know it. I have enrolled in Real Estate School. In a few months I should have my license and start selling houses, I hope. You know me, always planning for the future. Mom and Dad say, Hi. We really hope that you take this time to reconnect with God. He still loves you, and so do we.

Love Always,

Jenny

Rob put the letter down on the bunk next to him, leaned forward and stared at the floor. Tears streamed down his cheeks and splashed on the concrete floor between his feet. "My boy took his first steps. I should have been there," he sobbed softly.

The next day, Rob walked the exercise yard with Kurt and another White Power inmate. At the other end of the yard, Rob noticed several inmates entering one of the buildings. "What's that?" asked Rob as he pointed toward the building.

"What? Oh, that? That's the Chapel," answered Kurt.

"Chapel?"

"Yeah, where the weaklings go… you ain't no weakling, man, are you?"

"I might go check it out," pondered Rob out loud.

"You one of them… Holy Rollers?" laughed Kurt, shaking his head.

Later that evening, Rob paced back and forth like a caged panther in his cell. A look of anguish absorbed his face until he heard Correctional Officer Smith making his rounds. The prisoners called him Smitty to his face. Tall, thin, with a crop of unruly gray hair on his fifty-year-old head, Smith placed a check mark by each prisoner's name as he passed by their cell. He approached Rob's cell, they made eye contact, Smith put a check mark next to Rob's name, and then tucked the clipboard under his arm.

"C.O. Smith," whispered Rob. "C.O. Smith."

"What is it, Jacobs?" asked Smith as he approached Rob's cell.

"C.O. Smith, I need to see the chaplain," he softly muttered.

"Chaplain? You need to fill out a form for that. Can't it wait until Sunday?"

"No, sir, I need to see him right away."

C.O. Smith shook his head, and then handed Rob a form between the bars. "Here, Jacobs. Fill this out. I'll pick it up when I come back through. I'll turn it in for you."

"Thanks, Smitty," chimed Rob as he took the form from the Correctional Officer.

CHAPTER 24

The Chaplain's Clerk

The chaplain's clerk, Doc Burns, sat at his desk in the lobby of the chapel. Doc was only a nickname that he received for helping a midwife perform abortions. After several years, and countless abortions, he finally realized that what he was doing was wrong. He asked the Lord for forgiveness, repented and became a follower of Jesus Christ. Doc still had to pay for his crimes, but now he was a new creation in the Lord. He ran the fingers on his right hand through his white hair. In his left hand he held several papers. The old, round spectacles hung on the edge of his nose as he looked at the calendar on his desk. Rob entered and stood quietly at attention in front of him.

"Can I help you?" asked the clerk.

"Yes, sir, are you the chaplain's clerk? I have an appointment to see him and —"

"Hold your horses, sonny. Yes, I'm the chaplain's clerk and you are? Let me guess… Jacobs. Jacobs, right? 2:00 p.m.."

"Yes, sir, that's right. Is the chaplain here?" asked Rob nervously as he looked around.

"Simmer down, youngster. He's with somebody right now. Have a seat over there," ordered Doc Burns pointing to an empty chair up against the wall.

Rob sat in the chair and watched the clock on the wall behind the clerk's desk. Several minutes passed and Rob grew more impatient with every tick of the clock. The door to the chaplain's office finally opened and an inmate walked out. Rob anxiously stood up at attention as the inmate passed in front of him. Their eyes briefly met, and Rob recognized the inmate as Ben Richardson. They nodded to one another and Ben left the chapel.

"Okay, who's next, Doc?" asked Chaplain Parker, a short stocky man, with black hair, graying at the temples, wearing a black suit and tie.

"Oh, we got Jacobs, Rob Jacobs, here," stated Doc Burns pointing to Rob who was still standing at attention.

"Right this way, Jacobs," ordered Chaplain Parker, who turned and walked back into his office. Rob followed close behind and stood at attention while Chaplain Parker took his seat behind the grey metal desk.

"Sir, I'm Rob Jacobs, sir. I—"

The chaplain interrupted him and extended his hand. Rob reached out and shook the chaplain's hand. "Pull up a chair, Jacobs. Now, what can I do for you, son?"

Rob sat down and pulled his chair closer to the chaplain's desk. "Well… nothing. I just wanted—"

"A Bible? You want a Bible?" interrupted Chaplain Parker.

"Uh, yeah, sure. I'd like to have a Bible, but that's not why I came. I—"

"Yes, you what?" prodded the chaplain impatiently.

"I wonder… is it possible, you could contact my wife?"

"Contact your wife? Have you tried writing her a letter?"

"Yes, she wrote to me too, but I wanted to find out if she's really okay. You see, I'm worried about her and the baby."

"No, I am not allowed to contact your wife unless there is an emergency or something. It's against the rules."

"Oh, I didn't know—"

"Look, son, your wife can come visit you on Visitor's Day if she wants."

"I don't want her to see me in here, like this."

"Well, then there's nothing I can do for you then, except pray."

Rob sat in his chair with a frustrated and confused look on his face. "I don't know why I came here. I'm sorry," he said as his eyes filled with tears. "You know, I missed my son's first steps. I—" he added as he rose to leave.

"Wait a minute. Wait a minute, Jacobs," consoled Chaplain Parker softly. "Sit."

Rob sat back down in the chair and hung his head.

"Your first name is Robert, is that right? Rob? Rob. Let me ask you, are you a Christian, Rob?"

Rob hesitated to answer and the chaplain continued, "Let me ask you this: if you were to die today do you know where you would spend eternity?"

"Hell, I guess?"

"Not sure?"

"I'm not sure about anything these days. I became a Christian when I was in high school, but I haven't been a religious person."

"Religious person? Rob, it's not about being religious, it's about having a relationship. It's about our relationship with Jesus Christ."

"I don't have a relationship with anybody these days."

"Here, take this Bible. Read it. It is filled with personal letters to you from God. Just to you... personally."

Rob took the Bible from the chaplain and stood up. "Thank you, sir. I promise I will read this."

"Son, you can come back any time and talk to me. Hope to see you in the chapel this Sunday."

Rob walked out into the chapel lobby and passed Doc Burns, who was seated at his desk. "See you Sunday, Jacobs," smiled Doc Burns and he nodded at Rob as he left.

Every day Rob could be seen sitting on the edge of his bunk reading the Bible that Chaplain Parker had given him. Passages he had read as a teenager now took on a new, deeper meaning, as if written just to him and for his own personal benefit.

Correctional Officer Smith made his evening bed checks, counted heads and made sure everyone was accounted for. He often stopped by Rob's cell to see how he was doing. "Jacobs. Time to get some shuteye. It's late."

"Okay, Smitty. Just a few more minutes," begged Rob with the enthusiasm of a child watching his favorite show.

"All right, but just a few more minutes," relinquished C.O. Smith. "Got the GOOD BOOK there, huh?" he confirmed. "Well, that's good, but when I come back by here, it's lights out."

CHAPTER 25

Confrontation

Rob and Doc Burns took their daily walk around the track in the prison exercise yard. The exercise yard was busier than normal. It was the size of a football field without the goal posts. A couple dozen inmates jogged around the track counter-clockwise, while several others seemed to be out for a casual stroll. The weight pile was dominated by the muscular black inmates, while the whites and Latinos waited for their turn to pump iron. Rob was often intrigued by a separate, segregated part of the prison that had a foreboding look. "What's that over there, Doc?"

"That? That's Del Norte. You don't want to be in there, man," warned Doc Burns.

"Why? What is it? Maximum Security?"

"Somethin' like that. That's where they put all them drag queens, homos, and dope fiends."

"Why all the security? It looks like it's for serious offenders."

"You ain't heard of Del Norte? Two hundred and fifty men in there, with HIV, AIDS!"

"AIDS? Kinda like the lepers in biblical times, huh?" remarked Rob as he looked back over his shoulder at the notorious section of the prison, Del Norte.

"You know, Rob, I'm gonna be leavin' this place in a few weeks? Going to go live with my daughter and her husband in Fresno."

"Leaving?" said Rob in disbelief.

"Chaplain Parker's gonna need a new clerk. If you're interested, I can put in a good word for you with him?"

"Yeah, that would be great. Thanks Doc," said Rob as the two walked past the weight pile where several black inmates were lifting weights. Three of them stopped lifting, walked over and blocked Rob and Doc's path.

Booker was their leader: a thirty-year-old giant with biceps as big as the average-man's thighs. His shaved head glistened with sweat in the hot afternoon sun.

"Where you two sissy boys goin'?" challenged Booker angrily.

Doc Burns took a hard swallow, "We ain't lookin' for no trouble."

"Shut up, old man!" growled Booker who grabbed Doc by the lapels and pulled him close. "If you know what's good for you!"

"Let him go, NOW!" ordered Rob forcefully.

Booker released his grip on Doc and pushed him away, almost knocking him down. He turned and faced Rob, nose-to-nose, ready to fight. Booker raised his fist as if to throw a punch when suddenly a hand reached in and grabbed Booker's clenched fist. "Leave 'em alone, Booker!" a deep, loud voice yelled.

"What! Who do you think you are? Why you stickin' up for this crackah?" bellowed Booker.

Ben Richardson stepped between the two, "I said, leave 'em alone, or—"

"Or what?" retorted Booker.

"You'll have to deal with me!" warned Ben.

Booker and his cronies sheepishly turned and walked back to the weight pile.

"I can fight my own battles. I don't need your help," stated Rob.

"Right, I forgot. You a bad ex-marine. War hero and all," mocked Ben.

"Gentlemen, I only got a few weeks to go and I'm outta here. I don't need all this macho stuff," counseled Doc Burns.

"Figured I owed you one, Jarhead," chimed Ben who turned and walked away while Doc and Rob continued on toward the chapel.

CHAPTER 26

Sunday Service

It was a bright, sunny, but chilly, Sunday morning. The small prison chapel buzzed like a beehive with anticipation for the morning service. Rob was one of the first to arrive and found a seat in the front row, directly in front of the podium. He was jostled by someone on his left, and turned to see Ben Richardson grinning back at him.

"What are you doing here?" asked Rob. "You gonna sit with the white boys? They already think that you're an Uncle Tom."

"Take a look around, Rob. What do you see?"

"A lot of convicts."

"Yeah, but this is the only place inside this whole prison where blacks, Hispanics and whites can sit together as one. United as brothers… in the Lord."

Rob looked around the chapel again and saw that Ben was right. Everyone was friendly, smiling, and some even shaking hands.

"You see? And that's the reason I got between you and Booker the other day," explained Ben.

The multi-ethnic inmate choir entered and stood before the prison congregation. The choir leader handed out copies of Amazing Grace and then took his position in front of the inmate choir with his back to the inmate congregation.

"You? A Christian? I would have never guessed in a thousand years," quipped Rob in Ben's ear as the chapel erupted with a loud rendition of Amazing Grace. Ben looked at Rob and they both smiled broadly. Chaplain Parker walked out carrying his Bible, took his position behind the podium, and began singing loudly, slightly off-key. Rob struggled with the meaning of the song and he began to question God's love for him once again. "Why would God love me, after all I've done?" he mumbled under his breath.

After the great hymn, Amazing Grace, was over, Chaplain Parker addressed his inmate congregation, "Gentlemen, please be seated. Amazing Grace. I must have sung that song a thousand times and it still touches my heart and soul. A fellow by the name of John Newton wrote that hymn. John Newton's mother died when he was about six years old. He was raised by his father, who was a professional sailor and absent most of the time. So, John, like many of you, fell in with the wrong crowd. He became a sinner, led into moral corruption by his so-called friends, and fell deeper and deeper into sin. Does that sound familiar, gentlemen? When John got a little older, he became a slave trader and brought slaves to the United Kingdom. He continued to fall deeper and deeper in sin until one day he hit bottom. Some Christians began witnessing to him and someone gave him a book called The Imitation of Christ, which he read. The book had an effect on John and it touched his heart. The Spirit of God had begun to work on him. Sometime later, John was out at sea during a raging, violent storm when a giant wave swept him right off the deck into the sea. He thought that the ship would sink and that he was a gonner too. But then another giant wave took him and splashed him right back down on that deck of that ship. It was that incident that motivated him to cry out for mercy and accept Jesus Christ as his Lord and Savior. John Newton became a great minister and preached against slavery whenever and wherever he could. He wrote that song, Amazing Grace. It's that amazing grace that has saved a wretch like you and me. Please take your Bibles and turn to Titus, Chapter 2, starting at verse 11. Can I get a volunteer to read verses 11 through 14?"

Ben Richardson raised his hand. "I will, Chaplain."

"Thanks, Ben. Go ahead," said Chaplain Parker.

Ben stood up, opened his Bible and began reading at verse 11, "Fo da grace of God dat bringeth salvation hath appeared unto all men, teaching us dat denyin' ungodliness an' worldly lusts, we should live soberly, righteously, an' godly in dis present world, lookin' fo' dat blessed hope an' da glorious appearing of da great God an' our Savior Jesus Christ who gave himself fo' us, dat he migh' redeem us from all iniquity an' purify unto himself a peculiar people, zealous of good works."

"Very good. Thank you, Ben. You may sit down," advised the chaplain. "That is what God's amazing grace is men. Let's sing that song again. Amazing Grace—"

Tears began to flow down Rob's cheeks, but he held back any real sobbing that would have happened had he let his guard down completely. He sang along with the other inmates and began to realize God's amazing grace in his own life.

CHAPTER 27

The Invitation

Jenny sat at the kitchen table with the baby, her mother, and stepfather, Joseph, eating lunch. Joseph had met Jenny's mother at an Alcoholics Anonymous meeting several years ago. Together they had battled the demon of alcohol and both had remained sober ever since the day they met. They were attracted to each other right away. If there was such a thing as love at first sight, then that was what happened to them. It was mutual. She was attracted by his rugged good looks: tall and slim, with sandy blond hair. He was drawn to her youthfulness: a curvaceous figure, outgoing personality and wit. But most importantly, both came to the personal knowledge that their higher power was in fact Jesus Christ.

In his highchair, the baby squished spaghetti through his fingers, and then ran them through his hair, creating a spiked tomato-red hairdo.

"Get the camera, honey," said Grandma to her husband.

"I need to send a picture to Rob," laughed Jenny. "Too funny for words."

Joseph returned with a camera and snapped several photos of the baby and the two women as they laughed.

"I got a letter from Rob yesterday. He wants me to visit him next Sunday," announced Jenny. "I'll bring him some pictures of the baby. He'll like that," Jenny added with a smile.

Jenny's mother and stepfather glanced at each other briefly, and then her stepfather set the camera down on the table with a thud. "You think that's a good idea?" he asked. "Giving him false hope and all?"

"False hope?" inquired Jenny.

"Well, dear, you're not going to let him back into your life are you?" quizzed her mother.

"We took an oath when we got married, mom. I promised I'd be there for him."

"That oath didn't mean too much to him, now did it?" asked Joseph.

"His letter said he has been reading the Bible and going to Chapel services," defended Jenny.

"Another so-called 'jailhouse conversion,'" replied Joseph, sarcastically.

"Well, I am going to go see him on Sunday," announced Jenny.

Her mother and Joseph did not say a word as they stared at one another, and continued to eat their lunch.

CHAPTER 28

The Visit

Rob sat across the desk from Chaplain Parker as the chaplain read Rob's request to be his new clerk.

"Rob, as you know, Doc has been released and he recommended you to replace him," said Chaplain Parker.

"I would like to have that job sir, if it's okay with you?"

"I normally look for someone who is more mature spiritually, Rob. I'm not sure."

"You won't be sorry, Chaplain. I'm a very hard worker."

"Well, Doc thought you'd be the one," said the chaplain with a long pause. "Okay, I'm sending in the paperwork requesting you as my clerk, but... there's going to be a probationary period involved. If you don't work out, you're gone, back to the laundry room," he warned.

"Fair enough. Thank you, sir. I won't let you down."

"Okay, back to your dorm. You'll be notified when it goes through."

"I can't wait to tell Jenny. I think she may come to visit me this Sunday."

"That's good, Rob," smiled Chaplain Parker.

Sunday mornings at the prison's visiting yard proved to be quite hectic, especially for visitors. First, Jenny had to show the guard at the reception desk valid picture identification, which she provided by a driver's license. Then her purse had to be emptied and the contents examined for contraband. Next, her person was searched by a female correctional officer, which proved to be embarrassing because of the wire support in her bra. Finally, she had to walk through a metal detector. Once cleared, she was allowed to follow several other visiting girlfriends, wives, mothers and a few children, who were escorted by a correctional officer to an area with a couple dozen-picnic tables. They were ordered to sit there and wait for their inmates, but they would only have a half-an-hour visit. Jenny looked around at all of the various types of visitors, which were mostly women and children. There were grandmothers, mothers, sisters, girlfriends, and wives. All of them were anxiously waiting for their loved-ones to arrive. Children played together, oblivious to their surroundings. Jenny looked in the direction of the cellblocks and waited.

Jenny's heart pounded in her chest like a bass drum when Rob approached the visiting area, escorted by correctional officers. When their eyes met, wide toothy smiles spread across their faces. They wanted to run to each other, but circumstances prevented that from happening. She and Rob had both been previously warned that hugging or kissing was prohibited.

Rob approached the picnic table and sat down across from Jenny. They simultaneously reached across the table to hold each other's hands, and both gazed lovingly into the other's longing eyes, which slowly filled with joyful tears. Even though they were surrounded by inmates, visitors and guards, it was as if it was just the two of them.

"I miss you so much, Jen. I'm so sorry. I've made a mess of everything."

"I miss you too," she said longingly as the ache in her heart intensified and traveled to the pit of her stomach.

"I promise, when I get out of here I will make it up to you, and the baby."

"Are you all right?" asked Jenny.

"I'm fine. I think that going to prison was the best thing that ever happened to me. Well, I mean… next to marrying you, and… the baby and all."

"Glad you cleared that up," she quipped.

"No, I mean, I am clean and sober. I've had time to think, time to read the Bible. I feel good about myself. I might be working as the chaplain's clerk. Do you know what I am trying to say?"

Jenny reached across the table and held Rob's hands. "Yes, I do. I'm proud of you."

"And you! I'm so proud of you! Getting your real estate license and all."

The loudspeakers made a squelching sound, and then a commanding voice made an announcement that visiting hours were over and that everyone would have to leave.

"We'll have a house of our own some day, you'll see," added Rob as he struggled to let go of Jenny's hand, but reluctantly pulled away.

"Okay, you two. You heard the man. Break it up. Visiting hours are over," announced a burly correctional officer that hovered over them. "Let's go, Jacobs. Back to your dorm," he ordered. "Lady, you have to go… now."

Jenny stood and lovingly gazed at Rob as he turned and got in line with the other inmates. She waved goodbye and walked with the other visitors toward the exit gate.

Officer Smith walked down the long hallway with a slip of paper in his hand. He approached Rob who was seated on the edge of his bunk reading the Bible.

"Jacobs!" yelled Smith. "Got some good news for you," he added, and handed Rob the piece of paper.

"Thanks, Smitty," said Rob as he took the paper and quickly read it. "I start tomorrow as the chaplain's clerk."

"Good for you, Jacobs. Good for you," said the old guard as he turned and walked away smiling.

CHAPTER 29

Prison Ministry

Rob sat at his desk, and surveyed his new surroundings. He felt a sense of pride and importance as he sifted through a pile of paperwork. Chaplain Parker bounded out of his office and handed Rob a letter. "Rob, this is a letter from an outside ministry called Prisoner's Fellowship. They are asking permission to do a marriage seminar in the chapel."

"Marriage seminar? How does that work?"

"It says that I would select several inmates that are good candidates for the seminar, and invite their wives to participate. The wives would come into the chapel on Saturday morning, leave in the afternoon, and then return Sunday after the morning service. It would conclude early Sunday evening when the inmates have to be back in their cells."

"That sounds great. Could I be a part of that?"

"Not sure I want to do it yet. I need to find out more, and also get permission from the warden. I know that each inmate and his wife have a volunteer mentor couple. And, at the conclusion, couples renew their marriage vows. You could help me pick the inmates, and send an invitation to their wives."

"I know my marriage could use some help, Chaplain."

"Well, don't get too excited about it. There's a mountain of red tape we'd have to go through. Let me look into this."

Warden Reichert was a tall, slender man, with slick dark-brown hair combed straight back. He sat in his oversized leather chair behind a huge mahogany desk reading the request from Chaplain Parker concerning the Marriage Seminar. Seated across from him was Captain Brenner, his top correctional officer. Brenner was an average looking guy, except for a scar that ran the length of his right cheek. He kept his uniform impeccable and his badge would blind you if it caught the sun just right.

"Warden, what's so amusing?" asked Brenner.

"This request from Chaplain Parker. HA!"

"He's not asking for one of those yard concerts again, is he?"

"No. A Prisoner's Fellowship Marriage Seminar. Seems he wants to bring in volunteers and conduct a two-day seminar in the chapel. Inmates' wives are part of it."

"What! No way. We don't have the extra officers to provide security."

"They want to bring in food too. And, a wedding cake. Ha!"

"Yeah, with a saw hidden in it no doubt. What is that Chaplain thinking?"

Warden Reichert paused and leaned way back in his leather chair. After thinking a few minutes, he said, "You know, it might be good... I think it might be good for the inmates that have a year or less on their sentence. I am a firm believer in marriage. Got to keep the family together. You know, Captain, it might be a good thing."

"Are you sure, sir? How you going to choose what inmates attend?"

"I'll leave that up to the chaplain. See if you have a few officers that would like to volunteer to work the chapel for this thing." The warden signed the paperwork approving the marriage seminar. "That'll be all, Brenner."

"Yes, sir," answered Brenner as he turned and left the room shaking his head in disbelief.

Jenny sat on the living room sofa and gazed out the window at the curbside mailbox. Her mother finished putting the breakfast dishes away, looked at Jenny and shook her head. "Jenny, looking out the window like that won't make the mail come any faster."

"Well it might!" Jenny laughed. "I just really hope I get a letter from Rob today," she sighed. Then suddenly jumping up she exclaimed, "See, Mom! There's the mailman now!" Jenny bounded out the door with the excitement of a teenager and ran to the mailbox. She anxiously looked through the mail for something from Rob as she walked back to the house.

"Anything from Rob?" asked her mother.

"No," she sighed, "but there's an invitation here from the prison chaplain."

"An invitation?"

"Yes, it says it's for a Marriage Seminar. Two days, Saturday and Sunday. Next month."

"A Marriage Seminar? What on earth?" puzzled Mom.

"I think this is just what Rob and I need. Something to get our marriage back on track, but—"

"If you're worried about the baby, Joseph and I will take care of him."

Jenny sat down at the kitchen table and stared at the invitation. She read it several times before she stopped and stared out into space.

CHAPTER 30

The Marriage Seminar

The day of the Marriage Seminar finally arrived. Eleven inmates sat nervously in the prison chapel pews and talked amongst themselves about the arrival of their wives. Ben Richardson was one of those inmates that squirmed in his seat with anticipation. Seated next to him, Rob nervously bit his fingernails.

"Won't be long now. Can't wait to see my wife," whispered Rob into Ben's ear.

"Thanks, Jacobs," replied Ben.

"For what?"

"Fo' recommendin' me fo' dis."

"You can thank Chaplain Parker. He's the one who made the final selection."

"Yeah, but you picked me first. I owe you big time."

In the back of the chapel stood Correctional Officer Smith, arms folded across his chest, keeping a relaxed eye on the selected group of inmates. *Never had one of these kind of seminars at the prison before,* he thought. *Going to be real interestin'.*

Jenny stood in line with eleven inmate wives and six volunteer couples from the prison ministry between two razor wire fences. The wives chattered nervously like a bunch of turkeys on Thanksgiving Day. The group entered a small reception room where a stoic Captain Brennen greeted them. "Okay folks. Can I have your attention?

These officers here are going to search your belongings, and then each one of you will go through the metal detector. You need to take off all of your jewelry, belts, shoes… anything that's made of metal. Place it in the plastic tubs."

Sandra Jefferson was a street-wise black woman from Compton who did not take to well to any kind of authority. She wore too much makeup and too little dress. "This is ridiculous," she said under her breath. "This is gonna take all day."

"Don't make a scene," pleaded Jenny. "You can ruin this for all of us."

"Well, I got wire in my bra. Do they want me to take that off?" said Sandra sarcastically.

Captain Brenner overheard Sandra's comments and walked up to her, "That won't be necessary, ma' am. Officer Charles will just wand you."

"Wand me? What is he, the tooth fairy or somethin'?"

Brenner walked away as Officer Charles passed the hand held metal detecting wand over Sandra. "Clean," announced Officer Charles.

"Clean? You bettah believe it suckah," said Sandra defiantly.

After all the wives and volunteers went through the process of having their identifications checked and being searched, they were led through the prison yard toward the chapel. They could hear whistles and catcalls from the inmates out on the exercise yard.

"Humph! Don't be ogling me. I'm a married woman!" exclaimed Sandra.

After the wives had reached the chapel, they were paired up with their husbands. It was hard for them to keep from hugging and kissing their mates, but Correctional Officer Smith was visibly upset. He made his way to the front of the chapel and stood behind the podium. "May I have your attention," he said with authority. "Even though we are in the chapel, we all have to obey the prison rules. That means there will be no hugging or kissing. Also, everyone has to stay together, here, in the chapel. Is that understood?"

There were a few moans and groans from husbands and wives. Ben Richardson stood up and shook his head. "No huggin' or kissin'? Come on, give me a break, Officer Smith."

"These aren't my rules. They're the rules of the Department of Corrections," countered Smith.

"Well, they oughta correct that rule," blurted out Sandra Jefferson.

"I'm going to turn it over to Chaplain Parker. He's arranged this whole thing," deferred Officer Smith.

Chaplain Parker walked to the podium as a thunderous applause erupted. "Thank you. Thank you. We all owe a debt of gratitude to Warden Reichert," said the chaplain. "I want to welcome all of the wives that are with us. And, the Prisoner's Fellowship volunteers. They will be the ones conducting this marriage seminar. This is Pastor Diaz, from Prisoner's Fellowship," said Chaplain Parker as he waved his left hand in the direction of the Pastor. "He will be leading the seminar, and of course you have already met your mentor couples. Pastor Diaz."

Pastor Diaz was a short Hispanic man with a bushy black mustache and jet black hair that was combed straight back. He had on a brown suit, white shirt, and an old wide tie with the colors of the Mexican flag. "Thank you, Chaplain. I want to thank Chaplain Parker, and also Warden Reichert for making this event possible. We will be trying to squeeze a three-day seminar into a day and a half. So, we'll be moving rather quickly."

Chaplain Parker stepped back up to the podium and took the microphone from Pastor Diaz. "Oh, before I forget. A little housekeeping items. One, we do not have a ladies' restroom here, so the ladies will use the staff restroom next to my office. Two, I won't be here all the time, but please obey the orders of C.O. Smith and the other correctional officers," said the chaplain, handing the microphone back to Pastor Diaz and sitting down in the front row.

"As I was saying, we will be moving rather fast. The inmates are allowed to stay in the chapel during lunch," advised Pastor Diaz. "We were allowed to bring in food, and tomorrow at the conclusion we will rededicate our marriage vows and have some wedding cake!" There were some scattered applause from the participants and volunteers as the Pastor continued, "We will be covering forgiveness, the definition of love, the roles of the husband and wife, and overall we'll be strengthening your marriage."

"Forgiveness," grumbled Sandra Jefferson as she glared at her husband Charlie. "That's gonna be a hard one for me."

Ben Richardson sat next to Sandra and heard what she said. He leaned over to his wife, Aleesha, and whispered lovingly in her ear, "You forgive me, baby, don'cha?"

Aleesha pulled her hand away from Ben's. Ben looked at her with a puzzled look on his face and was confused by her actions. Pastor Diaz observed the reactions from Sandra and Aleesha and tried to clear the air, "Okay, well… let's open the program with prayer." Pastor Diaz followed with a long, eloquent prayer involving love and forgiveness, but could see a degree of anger on some of the wives' faces. "Before we begin the seminar, I seem to detect an unforgiving spirit here. We should address that before going forward. Is there someone, one of the wives, that would like to come up and get it off her chest?"

Aleesha stood up, walked to the front, and snatched the microphone from Pastor's Diaz. "Give me that mic," she snapped. "FORGIVNESS! Well, you right, Pastor. I need to get this off my chest. How can I forgive somebody that left me and went off to jail? He made me a single parent, tryin' to raise three kids under five! Buy groceries, pay the utilities! The Rent! Not to mention I gotta pay the babysitter when I go to work, and then there's the transportation! I been cryin' myself to sleep every night because my man ain't there next to me. Forgiveness! You talk about forgiveness? No, I can't forgive this man!"

It was so quiet in the chapel that you could hear an angel's feather hit the ground. Suddenly, Sandra Jefferson jumped to her feet. Her husband, Charlie, tried to grab her hand and pull her back to her seat, but it was too late. "That's right! You go, girl. Tell 'em. They is no good, dirty dawgs!" she yelled.

Pastor Diaz, afraid things were rapidly getting out of hand tried to take the microphone away from Aleesha, but found himself in an embarrassing tug of war, which Aleesha won. "Ben, I don't know if I can forgive you," she said into the mic, glaring at her husband. "You got three meals a day, a place to lay your head. You got everything you need. But you know what I need? I need to hear you say that you are sorry, Ben."

Ben stood up with his arms stretched out wide. Tears streamed down his cheeks like swollen streams. "Baby, I'm so sorry. I had no idea what you been goin' through. You... and the kids. Please forgive me."

"That's what I mean, Ben. You had no idea what I been dealin' wit. No idea... and that's because you only been thinkin' 'bout yo'self!"

"Baby, I'm sorry," pleaded Ben.

Pastor Diaz was finally able to snatch the microphone away from Aleesha, and gave her a gentle push in the direction of Ben. Chaplain Parker looked as though he was in shock. He stood up, walked over and stood next to Pastor Diaz. "Well... thank you, Aleesha. Uh, please have a seat next to Ben there," said the Pastor. "I, uh... see we have some issues to work through, especially in the forgiveness department. Is there anyone else?" said the Pastor as he glanced at one of his volunteers, Ed Barnes, and nodded in the direction of a table that contained the seminar materials. "Now, Ed and his wife, Shirley, are going to pass out the booklets and materials. As long as nobody else has something to say... we need to get started."

Rob stood up and turned to Jenny. Pastor Diaz and Chaplain Parker looked at each with nervous anticipation. Rob continued, "I just want to tell my wife that I am truly sorry for everything. I love you, Jenny."

"I love you too, Rob," she said softly.

"Forgive me?" he asked.

"No. Not yet," she said as a matter of fact.

Pastor Diaz, sensing the tension in the room, interrupted, "Okay... okay... let's get started, shall we?" he said as he looked around the room, and noted that all of wives appeared to be miffed at their spouses. "Please open your books to the first chapter,

Forgiveness. We are also going to be using our Bibles, so if you don't have one hold up your hand and Shirley will get you one."

After Shirley handed out a few Bibles, Chaplain Parker went to the podium and stated, "It looks like you got everything under control. I'll leave everyone in the good hands of Pastor Diaz and the volunteers. I'll be in my office." The chaplain nodded at the Pastor and left the chapel.

"Finish reading the first chapter in the book, then team up with your mentors and discuss what you learned, and so on," directed Pastor Diaz.

The rest of the day went according to plan and the inmates and their spouses worked with their volunteer couple. Time flew by and the day was over before they knew it. Several correctional officers arrived at the chapel and escorted the inmates back to their cells. Correctional Officers Smith and Garcia escorted the wives and volunteers out of the prison. Once the volunteers and wives were in the parking lot, Pastor Diaz reminded everyone to be punctual and meet on time the following day in the parking lot. If anyone was late they would not be admitted.

Everyone was on time the next day and everything went according to schedule. After lunch, the inmates and their wives sat close together in the chapel holding hands and looking very much in love. Pastor Diaz stood at the podium with microphone in hand. "I hope this has been a beneficial weekend for you. I know it has been a blessing for me and the volunteers," he said, and everyone nodded in agreement. "I have noticed that several of you have worked through the issue of forgiveness. Yes, it's good to see all of you holding hands. In love," he added with a huge smile. "In a few moments we will renew our wedding vows and have some cake. But in a while, the volunteers and your spouses will be leaving. Reality sets in, and you are back in your cell, incarcerated in this prison. I encourage you to stay grounded in God's word. Go back and read your seminar materials. You'll be back home sooner than you can imagine. Now, Sister Shirley is going to bless us with a song."

Sister Shirley sat at the shiny, black upright piano in the corner of the chapel and began to play. When she was done playing, Pastor Diaz asked everyone to stand and join hands with their partner.

"We know you all are married, but after a weekend like this we always renew our wedding vows," advised the pastor. "Gentlemen, please hold hands with your bride. In the coming decades you will be able to concentrate on building your love for each other. Of course, there will be tensions and worries involved in establishing yourselves financially and nurturing your love, but today we reassure each other that your love and trust is the basis for your marriage relationship. A relationship of a husband and wife that's full, with a deep bond that unites you both. The stresses and tensions of the past have not yet weakened your love, but have only made you determined to stick by each other. This relationship is and must be very deep. This afternoon's ceremony should encourage you both to be more dedicated to each other. And, you can look forward to a settled and enjoyable future together. Now, gentlemen, repeat after me, I, state your name—"

In unison all the men replied, "I, state your name—"

"No, no," said the Pastor. "Say your first name." There were a few chuckles from the group, then the pastor continued, "Take you... state your wife's name, to be my lawful wife, to have and to hold from this day forward, for better, for worse, for richer, for poorer, in sickness and in health. This day I affirm that vow."

The men repeated the pastor's words and there was an awkward silence, which was broken by the heavy sobs of Sister Shirley, "I always cry at weddings," she confessed.

"Now the wives. Repeat after me. I, state your name, take you as my lawful husband, to have and to hold from this day forward, for better, for worse, for richer, for poorer, in sickness and in health. This day I affirm this vow," said Pastor Diaz. The wives repeated the pastor's words and some began to softly weep. "I now pronounce you husband and wife. You may kiss your brides."

Everyone hugged and kissed their spouse, including the married volunteers. "Let's cut the cake!" yelled Pastor Diaz, and a loud cheer went up from everyone. They all gathered around the table and the pastor cut the wedding cake with a plastic knife.

Later that night, Rob sat alone in his cell writing a letter to Jenny. As he was writing, he unwittingly spoke aloud, "Jenny, this was the best weekend of my life. I know a lot of healing has taken place. Thank you for forgiving me. I hope I can be the husband you deserve. I have just a year left on my sentence and then I'll be home. I love you so much. I can't wait to be home with you and our son, Michael." A correctional officer walking past Rob's cell, paused to listen, then continued down the hall. "You'll be back," he predicted with a cynical laugh.

—

Warden Reichert sat behind his big mahogany desk reading the weekend's reports. He stopped for a moment, and then pushed a button on his phone that activated the intercom for his secretary, Mrs. Rogers. Mrs. Rogers was an elderly white haired woman, well beyond the age of retirement, but being a widow without any children, this job was her life and she loved it.

"Mrs. Rogers… get Captain Brenner in here. I want his report on that Marriage Seminar we had over the weekend." "Oh, yes sir, Warden," she answered as she grabbed her telephone and began dialing Captain Brenner's extension.

As soon as Brenner got the message he hustled over to the warden's office and was standing at attention in front of Mrs. Roger's desk. "Good morning, Captain," she said. "Go right in. The warden's waiting for you."

Captain Brenner nodded, and then walked briskly into the warden's office. "You wanted to see me, sir?" he asked nervously.

"Yes Captain, I want your report on that Marriage Seminar. Anything out of the ordinary happen?"

"No, sir. Everything went smoothly. My men said it was fine. No problems."

"Good! Put it in writing and give it to Mrs. Rogers before the end of watch. I'm glad things went well."

CHAPTER 31

Doubts

Chaplain Parker sat at his desk across from Rob who was holding a pad and pencil. "Glad to hear that everything went well over the weekend. Makes it easier to have another one down the road with other inmates and their wives," said the chaplain. "Be hard for the warden to deny us now," he added.

"Chaplain, I've been studying and reading my Bible and I... I still have a lot of questions. Like war for example, why does God allow wars, killing?"

"Rob, men have been asking that question for thousands of years. Why does he allow Christians to hurt? We may never know the answer to why, but what we cannot see or understand about the 'why' is known by God. We lack His perspective. God can see into the future. We cannot. However, we have to have faith that the future is good, that His plan is good."

"I don't know, Chaplain. I guess I still have a lot of doubts. I don't understand why I have to go through so much?"

"All I can tell you, Rob, is that He has promised us that He will not allow our burdens to be more than we can bear. Trust in Him."

"That's harder than it sounds. Thanks, Chaplain."

"Just keep in the Word, keep studying."

Rob left the chaplain's office and walked across the exercise yard toward his unit. Unbeknownst to him Chaplain Parker watched him through his office window until he reached his destination. The chaplain then sat down, picked up his Bible and began reading.

Officer Smith was making the evening rounds and paused at Rob's cell. "Hey, Jacobs. You're always in that book. Learn anything?"

"Oh, yeah. I've learned a thing or two, Smitty."

"You've got less than a year to do on your sentence. Have you made any plans about what you're going to do when you get out?"

"No, not really. I haven't given it much thought. Seems so far away."

"Be here before you know it, sonny," said Smitty as he turned and continued his rounds.

Rob looked at the calendar hanging on the wall of his cell. *Still a long ways off,* he thought as he tried to rub the pain out of his leg.

CHAPTER 32

The Mail

The bathtub overflowed with huge sudsy bubbles as the sound of a squeaky rubber ducky was drowned out by baby Michael's laughter. Jenny grinned from ear to ear in delight; this was her and the baby's favorite time of the day. Bath time.

Jenny's mother stuck her head in the bathroom and laughed at the sight of her grandson enjoying his bath. "I'm not sure who is wetter, you or him," she giggled as the baby reached for his floating yellow rubber duckling.

"His daddy will be coming home soon," smiled Jenny. "We will all be together and be a family."

"That reminds me, the mailman dropped off a letter from Rob today."

The baby screeched with laughter and splashed sudsy water in Jenny's face. "Okay, Buster! You're outta there!" chuckled Jenny.

"Looks like you got your hands full with that one," laughed Mom.

"Did you say, I have a letter from Rob?"

"Yes, I put it on the kitchen table. You also got something from a Felix—"

"Werner? Felix Werner? That's Rob's old boss."

Jenny took baby Michael out of the tub, wrapped him in a large bath towel and vigorously dried him off. He tried to waddle away, but Jenny managed to hang on to one arm and corral him while she put on his diaper.

She went into the kitchen, opened Rob's letter and read it aloud so her mother could hear: "Dear Jenny, I am looking at the calendar in my cell and can't believe that I only have seven months left to serve. That seems like an eternity to me in here. I can't wait to come home and be with you and Michael. Part of me is afraid, though. Afraid of the unknown, afraid of failing again. Chaplain Parker tells me that I must have faith. It's hard, especially when I am full of fear about the future. I look forward to seeing you, holding you, and kissing you. I love you so much." Jenny held the letter to her bosom and smiled. She set Rob's letter down on the table and picked up the one from Felix Werner. She read it quietly to herself and when finished began to cry.

"What is it, dear? What's wrong?" asked Jenny's mother.

"It's Mr. Werner, mom. He's had a stroke."

"Oh, I'm sorry, honey," said her mother as she hugged Jenny tightly.

"The letter is from his sister. She says he is in the hospital. I have to go visit him," Jenny said with deep concern.

Jenny left the baby with her mother and went directly to the hospital. When she arrived at the Intensive Care Unit, she was directed to his room. Through the open doorway she saw that Felix was sitting up in bed and joking with one of the nurses. "Felix, you gave me a scare," said Jenny. "I've been praying constantly since I got the letter from your sister."

"Jenny, I'm fine," he said. "They are going to release me tomorrow."

"What a relief and an answer to prayer!"

"What's happening with Rob?"

"My mother says my marriage won't last. I just don't know."

"Well, Jenny, you are the one always quoting scripture. What does the Bible say?"

For once, Jenny was at a loss for words. Felix just smiled at her and waited.

"I… I don't know," she said.

"I am sure you have read that in the beginning the Creator made them, male and female, and said, 'For this reason a man will leave his father and mother and be united to his wife, and the two will become one flesh.' So, what God has joined together, let not man separate."

"Thank you, Felix."

CHAPTER 33

The Physical

Chaplain Parker sat at his desk reading a memo from Warden Reichert. When he finished it he sat it down on his desk. "Rob, can you come in here for a moment?" he called. Rob was at his desk in the lobby area and heard the chaplain call him. He stopped what he was doing and entered the chaplain's office, pulled out a chair and sat down.

"What can I do for you Chaplain?"

"Rob, I got a memo here from the warden. It says that you are required to have a pre-release physical six months prior to your release date. You are ordered to appear tomorrow at the prison hospital, 8:00 a.m. sharp."

"Pre-release physical?"

"Everybody has to have one. I just can't believe that you have only six months left on your sentence. You know, Rob, I'm really gonna miss you," he said softly, his voice tailing off. "Here are your orders. Says for you not to eat anything in the morning."

Rob nervously squirmed in the waiting room chair while he filled out some paperwork that the heavyset male nurse had given him. Several other inmates struggled filling out their forms and talked amongst themselves for obvious answers. Rob checked the large round clock on the wall for the fourth time in five minutes.

"Jacobs! Are you through filling out those forms?" barked the burly nurse.

"Uh, yes, I just have to sign here."

"Well, sign the stupid thing and get your butt up here," ordered the nurse. "We ain't got all day."

Rob signed the forms, jumped up, quickly walked to the counter, and handed them to the grouchy male nurse. The nurse perused the documents, took a long pause, and handed them back to Rob. "What? Did I forget something?" inquired Rob.

"Right there! You didn't check that box. Yes or No? Check one!" he snapped as he tapped the form in Rob's hand with a pencil.

"I don't think I need to be tested for that," stated Rob as he attempted to hand the form back to the nurse.

"Mark NO then, but if you got a family to go home to you might want to be tested."

Rob placed a mark on the form and handed it back to the nurse who glanced at it and set it down on his desk.

"Go back and have a seat. We'll call you in just a minute."

Rob went back to the plastic gray waiting room chair. After several minutes, the nurse came out and escorted him back to an examining room where he waited several more minutes. Finally, after what seemed like an eternity, the doctor entered. He was a skinny, hunched-back, old Caucasian man with wispy white hair, and thick black-rimmed glasses. The upper left-hand corner of his white coat read, "S. Layton, M.D." in cursive black letters.

"Jacobs, huh? I'm Doc Layton. I'll be giving you your physical today," he said as a matter-of-fact. "Let's see… it says here you were wounded in the Persian Gulf War. Is that correct? Any other wounds or injuries I should know about?"

"No, sir,"

"Fine. Okay, take off your clothes and slip into this hospital gown."

Rob disrobed and placed his clothes on a chair in the examining room. He put on the gown, but seemed embarrassed by the opening in the back. "Okay, Doc, ready."

The doctor placed the blood pressure cuff on Rob's left arm and noticed some scarring on his inner arm. "Intravenous drug user, huh?" announced the doctor.

"What?"

"Needles. You shot up? Drugs?"

"Yeah, a little bit, but that was a long time ago."

"Okay...blood pressure's normal. 120 over 72," stated Doc Layton as he listened to Rob's chest with a stethoscope. "Heart sounds good. Lungs clear. You are not a smoker are you, Mr. Jacobs?"

"No sir."

"Nasty habit... and deadly. Okay, let's see that leg of yours. You still have pain with this?" asked Doc as he squeezed Rob's leg tightly.

"Yeah, OUCH... I do," blurted Rob.

"How about here?" Doc asked as he squeezed the leg a little lower toward the ankle.

"Ouch! Geez! That hurts!"

"You receive any injuries during your incarceration?"

"Nothing to speak of."

"Okay, the nurse will be right in to take some blood from you. Just relax, it will be a few minutes."

The doctor wrote something on Rob's chart and left the room. Shortly, a nurse joined Rob and took some blood from his arm. "Have a seat in the waiting room. A correctional officer will escort you back to your dorm," said the nurse as he tossed Rob his clothes. "Just put that gown in the laundry basket."

Rob got dressed and returned to the waiting room. He sat staring at the clock until the guard came to take him and the other inmates back to their respected cells. He felt pretty good about all the tests. *I feel pretty healthy*, he thought. *I just can't wait to get out of this place and be with my family.*

CHAPTER 34

The Results

Chaplain Parker whistled an old hymn as he walked up and down the pews of the tiny chapel picking up hymnals, papers and trash that were left behind by inmate worshippers. Rob entered through a side door and approached the chaplain.

"You shouldn't be doing that, Chaplain, let me do that," stated Rob as he began picking up trash from under the pews.

"Oh, that's okay. Rob, I don't mind doing it."

"Yeah, but that's my job, Chaplain."

"Well, just don't call the union on me, that's all," laughed Chaplain Parker.

"Chaplain, I want to thank you for giving me this job. I've learned a lot from you and—"

"Whoa, there Rob. You're not going soft on me now, are you? Don't forget... once a tough marine, always a tough marine!" laughed the chaplain.

"Right! Semper Fi!"

"Always faithful, right Rob?"

"God is," answered Rob. "Chaplain, I just want you to know that I have asked the Lord back into my heart, and I've promised to serve Him the rest of my life."

"That's great news, son."

"I think I want to go to seminary when I get out. I think that God's calling me to be a pastor."

"Well, now, I think you'd be a wonderful pastor," said Chaplain Parker. "But, you got to be a little crazy to be a prison chaplain," he laughed.

The chaplain and Rob laughed as they continued to clean up the chapel. Just then the phone in the chaplain's office rang. "Got to get that, Rob. Be right back," he stated as he bounded toward his office.

The chaplain snatched the phone off of the receiver on the fifth ring and answered with a breathy "Hello, Chaplain Parker."

"Chaplain, Doc Layton here, glad I caught you. I wanted to tell you first, seeing that he's your clerk and all."

"Tell me what, Doc?"

"Your clerk, Rob Jacobs. He tested positive for HIV. He's got to be moved immediately to Del Norte."

"Are you sure?"

"Yes, no doubt about it. Sorry, Chaplain."

Stunned, Chaplain Parker sank quietly down into his desk chair. Tears welled up in his eyes and he stared up at the ceiling. "God, I don't understand, but I know you must have a reason for this," he whispered. After several minutes he called Rob into his office.

"You called, Chaplain? What can I do for you?"

"Have a seat, Rob."

"What's the matter, Chaplain? You look like you ate some bad sushi or something," Rob chuckled, but then stopped short when the chaplain just stared back at him with sad eyes.

"There's no easy way to tell you, Rob. That was Doc Layton on the phone. Your blood tests came back showing that you are HIV positive."

"What?! HIV positive? How can that be?!"

"Most likely from doing drugs. Sharing dirty needles? Who knows for sure? The thing is… you tested positive. You have been transferred to Del Norte."

CHAPTER 35

Del Norte

Sgt. Sharky and two other correctional officers walked briskly down the cellblock and came to an abrupt halt at Rob's cell. Sharky peered into the dimly lit cell and could see that Rob was sound asleep. "Jacobs! Rise and shine, jarhead!"

Rob jumped to his feet and stood at attention, still groggy and not quite awake. "Sir, Sergeant Sharky, sir! Is it time?"

Sharky motioned for one of the officers to open the cell door, and took a step back. "Let's go, Jacobs. Grab your personal crap and let's go!"

"Del Norte?"

"Come on, jarhead. We ain't got all day. Move it!"

Rob hastily grabbed all his personal belongings, put them into an empty pillowcase and followed the officers and Sgt. Sharky down the hallway. The other inmates began catcalling as they moved toward the cellblock exit. "You're going to the hole, Jacobs! Busted! What did you do this time, Jacobs?"

Ben grabbed the bars on his cell door and watched intently as Rob was escorted out of the cellblock.

Sharky and the two other officers walked Rob across the prison yard to a section that was surrounded by a forty-feet high chain link fence topped by two rows of razor wire. Behind the fence were three large gray buildings. On one were the words DEL NORTE.

As they approached the gate, Rob became apprehensive, and began to balk at entering. Sharky grabbed his arm tightly and assisted him through the gate.

"I'm supposed to be at my job in the chapel this morning," announced Rob.

"You got a new job now. You need to report to Doctor Chan," advised Sharky as he handed Rob over to another prison guard just inside the gate to Del Norte. "He's all yours. Take care of him; he's a good man," added Sharky.

Rob was led by the arm into the largest of the three gray buildings. The smell of a cleaning compound and a sickening medicinal aroma made him nauseous. The guard escorted him to Doctor Chan's office, opened the door and advised him to sit in an empty chair across from a large mahogany desk. "Doctor Chan will be with you in a minute," the guard advised.

Rob looked around the room and noted several diplomas and award plaques on the wall behind the shiny desk. Suddenly, the door abruptly swung open and banged against the wall. A short, stocky Chinese man in his mid-sixties bounded into the room and quickly took his position in a black leather chair behind the desk.

"Good morning, Mr. Jacobs. Welcome to Del Norte," said the doctor as he flopped a file down on the desk with loud snap. "You are here, Mr. Jacobs, because you tested positive for HIV."

"Ya, I heard that, but that can't be right. There's got to be some mistake," begged Rob.

"No mistake, Mr. Jacobs. I have your test results right here," he stated, opening Rob's file. "Yes, right here. Positive for HIV. You will now be residing in dorm A. Dorm B has more advanced cases of HIV, and men… dying, you know… of AIDS."

Rob sat absolutely motionless. He was stunned, and completely zoned out while the doctor continued talking; his voice sounded as though he were a million miles away.

"This is a bad dream. I'm dreaming, right? A freakin' nightmare."

"No dream. Reality, Mr. Jacobs, reality. Look on the bright side, you only have six months left on your sentence, right? Then you'll be going home."

"A nightmare—"

"Officer Garcia will escort you to your new dorm. Garcia!"

"Let's go, Jacobs," ordered Garcia.

Officer Garcia took Rob by the arm and led him to a stairwell and up to the first floor. They entered a large open room that had 4-foot high dividers that separated each inmate's living space. Each space was equipped with a bunk, a small desk area with a fold up chair, and a three-foot high wooden locker to store personal items.

"This is your bunk right here," Garcia pointed out.

"Where is everybody?" asked Rob.

"Either at chow or working," answered Garcia. "Did you have chow this morning?"

"No, I'm not hungry."

"You get a brown bag for lunch here at Del Norte, and you're about three hours away from that," stated Garcia. "I hear you're working for Doc Chan. He's a good man. You're lucky."

"Oh, yeah. Lucky. That's me."

"Just put your stuff away and come with me. I'll give you a little tour of Del Norte."

Rob emptied the pillowcase containing his personal belongings onto the bed, and then put them into his new wooden locker. He then followed Garcia back down the staircase to the main floor.

"Everybody in your building has some stage of HIV. You look pretty healthy to me, so you must be at the beginning stages?" queried Garcia as they walked down a long hallway. "Over here, that's the dining hall. The kitchen is back there. This room is being used as a chapel. Now, across the hall, over there, those three rooms are all classrooms. If you don't have a job, you have to attend classes. But, since you'll be working with Doc Chan—"

"What exactly will I be doing for Doc Chan?"

"That's up to him. I'm not sure. Come on, follow me."

Rob walked alongside Garcia to the adjacent building. "What's this place?" asked Rob.

"This is building B."

Rob's jaw dropped as he looked around. It was like a mausoleum: still, quiet, and lifeless. "God. It is so quiet in here. It gives me the creeps."

There were thirty-two beds in all. Each bed had a patient-prisoner with advanced stages of AIDS. The room was totally silent in an eerie kind of way.

"They are too weak to talk. Several of 'em are near death. More die here than on Death Row," advised Garcia as he and Rob continued to slowly walk the length of the hospital ward. A few patients acknowledged Rob with a slight nod and a wry smile. By the time the two reached the end of the aisle, tears had welled up in Rob's eyes.

"God… where are you, now?" questioned Rob as tears trickled down his cheeks.

CHAPTER 36

Introductions

The evening meal in the dining hall was quite hectic. The echo factor in the large hall made the smallest noise sound double or triple in volume. Rob picked up a tray from the rack and made his way through the chow line. He wasn't sure if the food looked better than in the Main Yard or that he was just hungry. After searching the room he found a seat at an empty table and sat down to eat his meal. Several other HIV inmates rapidly joined him and there were no vacant seats left. Rob nodded at a black inmate directly across from him who was wearing an orange jump suit. He was tall and thin, about thirty-six years old.

"Hey brother, they call me Snoopy," said the black inmate as he extended his hand. Rob was slow to extend his hand and Snoopy withdrew his without making contact. "Afraid, huh? Think you'll catch somethin'? Listen brother, if you is here in Del Norte, I hate to be the one to break it to ya, but… you already got it!" laughed Snoopy hysterically.

"Sorry, man. My name's Rob Jacobs. You can call me Rob."

The two shook hands and Snoopy introduced the other inmates at the table. "That's Pedro, that's Bruce, and that's Greg." Rob nodded at each as they were introduced and they nodded back. "We all hang together," added Snoopy.

"Hi guys," stated Rob.

"Just so ya know, they don't call him Snoopy because he's into everybody's business. They call him Snoopy 'cause he look like that cartoon dawg!" laughed one of the inmates.

"In here, I'm the guy you come to if you want anything. Whatever it is, I can get it. For a price that is," laughed Snoopy. "Cigarettes? I'm your man. Chocolate? Hooch? Aspirin? Speed? You name it."

"Oh, uh, that's good to know. Thanks," said Rob.

Later that night, Rob sat at the desk in his cubical with a pencil and paper. He struggled to compose a letter to Jenny. "What am I going to tell her?" he said out loud. *Hi honey! How are you? I'm good. By the way, I'm HIV positive,* he thought. "What will she think?! Oh, God, what am I going to do?"

He crumpled up another piece of paper from the yellow legal pad and angrily tossed it into the trashcan. Another frustrated attempt at writing caused him to snap his pencil in half. "Jenny, I don't want to lose you," he cried as he sunk his head down into his folded arms over the desk.

After an hour he finally finished his letter. He folded it carefully and tucked it into a stamped envelope addressed to Jenny. Exhausted, he laid on his bunk and stared up at the ceiling, but he could not fall asleep.

CHAPTER 37

A New Day

After breakfast, Rob found his way to Doctor Chan's office. The door was wide open so he walked in and saw the doctor sitting behind his desk writing on a clipboard. Rob stood there at attention waiting for him to look up and acknowledge his presence. Without looking up, Doc Chan continued to write and stated, "I'll be with you in a moment, Jacobs."

"Jacobs, reporting for duty, sir."

"Just a minute, okay, let's see here—" mumbled Doc Chan as he pulled out a file with Rob's name on it and studied it for a few minutes. "Hmm... good. So, you were the chaplain's Clerk. Is that correct?"

"Yes, sir. Does Chaplain Parker come here... to Del Norte?"

"Twice a week."

"Funny... he never told me about this place."

"Jacobs, I'm short on nurses so you will be helping me over in building B. Since you're healthy and strong, I can use your assistance with the patients. You know, helping them turn over, eat, go—"

"Uhh... I don't think I'm the right guy for that, doc." interrupted Rob.

"Yes you are. You're the one. Remember, you are here because you are HIV positive. The only way you leave Del Norte is when you are released or... dead."

"You really know how to cheer a guy up, Doctor Chan."

"When I get through with this paperwork you can accompany me on my morning rounds on B ward. Have a seat, and here, read this while you're waiting," he said and he tossed Rob several brochures about HIV and AIDS.

After several minutes, Doc Chan rose from behind his desk. "Okay, Jacobs, follow me."

Rob closely followed the doctor to B ward. When they entered, Rob smelled a mixture of urine and breakfasts that had gone uneaten. It made his stomach a little queasy. He became anxious and dreaded the thought of having to work daily with these advanced AIDS patients, and even more becoming one of them.

As the two made their way from bed to bed, Rob was right by the doctor's side listening to every word. They stopped at a 40-year-old inmate's bedside. He was obviously in the advanced stages of the disease. His face was drawn; his cheeks sunken into his face; his eyes sunken into their sockets. Rob immediately thought of the old photographs he had seen of Holocaust survivors.

"Rob," said Doctor Chan, "I want you to meet Andy. Andy, this is Rob Jacobs, my new assistant."

"Are you a doctor, Rob?" asked Andy with a raspy whisper.

"No, I'm just helping Doctor Chan."

"Aren't you afraid you'll catch IT?" smirked Andy sarcastically.

"No. I've read up on it. I'm not afraid."

"Andy, Rob just tested positive for HIV," informed Doctor Chan.

"I see," replied Andy.

"Rob is going to turn you on your side so I can take a look at your back. Okay?"

"Sure. Be gentle with me, Rob."

Doctor Chan handed Rob a pair of latex gloves that he awkwardly put on. He then gently but firmly grabbed Andy and turned him on his side. Andy groaned slightly. Doctor Chan opened the back of Andy's hospital gown to display numerous tumors on Andy's back. Rob winced and had to turn his head to keep from looking.

"Rob, can you help turn Andy back over?"

Rob turned Andy back to his original position, and Andy once again groaned in pain.

"Well, how am I doing Doc?" asked Andy.

"Just fine, Andy. Just fine. You try to get some rest now."

"Rob, thanks. Will you come back and see me?" asked Andy.

Rob nodded in the affirmative and then followed Doctor Chan to the next bed where a 50-year-old, very thin black man with a medium Afro was propped up on pillows.

"Well, Mr. Robinson, how are we today?" asked Doctor Chan.

"WE ain't doin' too good, is we?"

"Feisty today, huh, Mr. Robinson?" quipped Doctor Chan.

"If I could get out of this bed I would Kung Fu your Chinese butt," growled Robinson.

"That's no way to talk to somebody who's trying to help you. Besides, what is my new assistant going to think?" asked the old doctor.

"Yeah, like I care. Why don't you go help Andy, that old homo over there? You can hold his hand while he dies. I don't need nobody. Let me be."

"I'll be back, Robinson. I'd like to listen to your heart and lungs," advised Doctor Chan as Robinson turned on his side away from him and Rob.

In the very next bed lay the youngest patient in B ward. He was a constantly coughing, 19-year-old, scrawny white kid with long blond hair and scraggily blond beard. Everyone called him Splinter.

"Hey, Doc Chan. What's happenin'?" chimed Splinter. "Who you got with you? A new recruit? Is that Tonto, Lone Ranger?" he laughed nervously, and then began coughing uncontrollably.

"Splinter here used to be a drummer in heavy metal band. Started shooting smack and speed. Got full-blown AIDS a year ago. He's got 2 more years to serve on his sentence."

"Hey, Splinter. Hang in there kid," said Rob.

"Yeah, dude, you hang in there too… and they'll hang us together. Ha, ha, ha… that's a joke!" coughed Splinter.

"Let me take a listen to your chest today," stated Doctor Chan as he pressed the stethoscope to Splinter's chest. Doc looked up at Rob and shook his head.

"Can you hear the beat, Doc?" asked Splinter.

Doctor Chan nodded his head and he and Rob went on to the next bed. He and Rob made the rounds and visited all the patients on the ward.

Back in his office, Doctor Chan took his seat behind his big mahogany desk. "Have a seat, Rob," he said. "Pull your chair right up here."

Rob pulled his chair up close to the desk opposite Doctor Chan. "Doctor Chan, what's the story with Andy? He doesn't look too good."

"I give him a couple of weeks at the most. He lost his lover to AIDS a few years ago and went a little bit crazy. He gave it to about 10 other men before he was arrested. Says he's ready to go, and made peace with his Maker."

"And, Robinson?"

"He tries to be a tough guy. He was an intravenous drug user. Heroin. He's got a few months. Don't know if he'll make it to his release date."

"And, that kid, Splinter?"

"I don't know. He seemed to rally, but now… pneumonia. Not too much I can do."

"Why don't they just let these men go home and die with some dignity, instead of dying in some prison, like Del Norte?"

"Rob, who is going to take care of them on the outside? Nobody. At least here they have us."

CHAPTER 38

B Ward

The smell of scrambled eggs and burnt toast permeated the mess hall in A ward where all of the inmates gathered for breakfast. The sound of a multitude of conversations reverberated like a small roar around the room. Rob was late, but found a seat at a table with Snoopy. Without saying a word, Rob set his tray on the table and began eating.

"Hey, Rob, how's it goin'? asked Snoopy. "Hear ya been over at B ward with Doc Chan, huh? Didn't touch any of 'em did ya?"

"I'm going to be working over there with the Doc."

"Not me. No way. You wouldn't catch me over there. All they got to do is sneeze or spit on you and whammo! Your HIV becomes full blown AIDS. You end up in one of those beds in B ward, and you is HISTORY."

Rob just shook his head and continued eating as Snoopy continued, "Rob, you need Snoopy to get you anything? You gotta want something?"

"No, I'm cool. Don't need a thing, but if I did… you're the man I'd come to," replied Rob as he and everyone else shoveled in their breakfast.

Doctor Chan was standing in front of the tall green filing cabinet putting away some patient files when Rob walked into the office. "Good morning, Doc," Rob chimed.

"Rob! I'm glad you're here a little early. I have to run over to Central. There's some kind of an emergency. I'd like you to go ahead and check on all the patients in B ward this morning."

"Anything in particular you want me to do?" asked Rob.

"No, just make sure everyone is comfortable and still breathing," advised the doctor. "There's only one nurse over there. You could always pull one out of A ward in an emergency. Play it by ear."

"Okay, no problem, Doc."

"I should be back before noon. If you have any trouble, give Officer Garcia a call. He's in the office at the end of the hall," advised Doc Chan as he grabbed his black medical bag and hurried out the door.

Rob walked down the hall and noticed that the door to Officer Garcia's office was wide open. He observed Garcia seated at his desk drinking a cup of coffee and reading the morning newspaper. "Good morning, Officer Garcia," blurted out Rob cheerfully.

"Hey, you startled me. Jacobs, right?"

"Sorry, I just wanted you to know that Doctor Chan went over to Central. Some kind of emergency or something. He told me to go over to B ward without him, but I wanted to make sure that was cool with you?"

"Yeah, sure. If you need me just pick up any phone and dial 4477 and I'll be right over."

Rob left Garcia's office and headed over to B ward. Upon entering, he removed a clipboard hanging on the wall. He stopped at each bed, and made notations on the patient's well being as he went. Now, he was at Splinter's bed. "Yo, Splinter! How's it goin' dude?"

"Not so good today, man. Havin' trouble breathin'," he whispered hoarsely.

"Oh, sorry, man," Rob said apologetically. "Is there anything I can do?"

"No, I'll be okay," coughed Splinter. "Where's Doc?"

"He'll be by this afternoon. He had some kind of emergency. Are you sure there is nothing I can get you?"

"You know... I'd really like to have a cigarette. Could you get me a Camel?" he coughed.

"I don't think that would be the best thing for you right now."

"Ya, it might kill me!" Splinter choked out.

"How'd you get the nickname...Splinter?" asked Rob.

"Duh! Are you slow or somethin'? I'm a drummer? Wooden drumsticks? Splinters? Get it?"

"Oh, now I get it," chuckled Rob

Splinter began a coughing jag, rolled over on his side away from Rob who determined this was a signal for him to move on to the next bed.

"Oh no, not you again? I thought you'd turn tail and run," exclaimed Robinson sarcastically.

"Nope. I'm still here," answered Rob. "Need anything?"

"Yeah, some wings so I can fly out of this coop," quipped Robinson. "What was your name again?"

"Rob, Rob Jacobs."

"Can you get me a glass of water, Rob Jacobs?"

Rob poured a glass of water from the picture on the nightstand and handed it to the inmate. Robinson took a few sips and handed it back to Rob.

"You're welcome," said Rob sarcastically.

"Didn't I say thank you?"

"Yeah, I know."

Rob smiled and went on to the next bed where the prisoner Andy was curled up in a fetal position. "Hi, Andy, how are you today?"

"You came back to see me," said Andy as he slowly turned over and looked at Rob.

"Yep, you're right. How are you today, Andy?"

"Tired, very tired."

"Is there anything that I can do for you?" asked Rob.

Andy slowly and painfully lifted his arm and pointed at the Bible on his nightstand. "Can you read to me?" he asked. "Just until I fall asleep?"

Rob picked up the Bible, opened it and began to leaf through its pages. "Sure, anything in particular?"

"Luke 17. Start at verse eleven," he replied in a soft, raspy voice.

Finding the chapter in the Book of Luke, Rob began to read aloud, "Now on His way to Jerusalem, Jesus traveled along the border between Samaria and Galilee. As he was going, ten men who had leprosy met him." Rob stopped reading and looked at Andy. "Oh, this is where Jesus heals the ten lepers. I know this one," stated Rob.

"Only one out of the ten came back and thanked him. He didn't heal me, but I thank him for saving me," declared Andy. "In awhile… I will have the ultimate healing. Read some more, Rob."

Rob continued to read the story of the ten lepers and finished with verse 19. "Rise and go; your faith has made you well."

Andy reached his hand out for Rob. "Will you hold an old gay man's hand?" whispered Andy. "Read me some more, Rob."

Rob compassionately took Andy's hand and continued reading the Bible. When Rob finished the chapter, he looked up at Andy and realized that Andy had quietly passed away. Rob closed the Bible with one hand and set it down on the nightstand, and then placed both of Andy's hands together on his chest. A tear trickled down Rob's cheek as he sat motionless, staring at the floor.

CHAPTER 39

Decisions

Jenny put the last spoonful of applesauce in the baby's mouth and tossed the jar into the trashcan. "You ate the whole thing, you little piggy," she said. "Look, Mom, he ate the whole jar. He's getting so big."

"Yes, he is," replied her mother. "The mail just arrived. It looks like you got something from Rob," she added as she handed the letter to Jenny.

Jenny took the letter and excitingly ripped it open. She sat in the kitchen chair and quietly began reading it to herself. "Oh my God," she gasped and the color drained from her face.

"What is it? What's the matter, dear?" asked her mother.

"Mom, I don't know what I'm going to do? Rob is HIV positive! They've transferred him to the AIDS section of the prison, Del Norte."

"Oh no... I'm so sorry honey... Well, I'm sure when he gets out he can find somewhere to stay... maybe a half way house or a clinic?

"What?! What do you mean?"

"Well, you can't have him back here, you know. You've got to think about yourself and about your baby."

"What do you want me to do? Forget all about him? He needs me now more than ever."

"You don't have a choice, Jenny. You need to divorce him now, before he gets out."

"I can't do that, Mom. I love him."

"Jenny, your father and I will help you. Joseph has a good friend who's a divorce attorney. It's the only way to keep you safe."

Jenny looked at the baby, and then back at her mother with a puzzled look on her face. "I don't know, mom. I just don't know."

CHAPTER 40

Death

Chaplain Parker sat at his desk where he prepared for Sunday's sermon when the telephone rang. It was Warden Reichert. Rarely did the chaplain have a direct call from the warden, unless it was bad news. "Hello, this is Chaplain Parker," he said.

"Chaplain, Warden Reichert here. I'm calling to let you know that one of the inmates in Del Norte passed away. Andrew Morrow. I'd like you to notify the next of kin, seeing he was one of yours. I believe you have all of his personal information, who to contact?

"Yes, I have all of that. I will take care of it. Thank you," said Chaplain Parker and hung up the phone. He got up from his desk and walked over to a tall filing cabinet. He opened the second drawer and removed a file with the name Andrew Morrow on it and returned to his desk. He opened the file and silently read its contents. He was interrupted when one of the prison guards entered his office. "Officer Jackson, what can I do for you today?"

Officer Jackson was a large black man, dark skinned, with a buzz cut and a neatly trimmed mustache. He was soft-spoken, but sometimes too quick to react. "Just thought I'd stop by to see how you're doing, Chaplain. You don't look too good. Are you sick?"

"Sick to my stomach. We lost another one in Del Norte to the Monster."

"Sorry, Chaplain. I wish they had better care… more doctors, nurses. You know."

"Yes. Doctor Chan and two nurses just aren't enough for two hundred and fifty men. Thirty, no, now twenty-nine men with advanced AIDS."

"Sad," stated Jackson who shook his head in distain.

"Sad? It's a down right travesty!" exclaimed the distraught Chaplain. "If you could excuse me, Jackson, I have to make a Death Notification."

"Sure, Chaplain, sorry," said Jackson who turned and walked out of the room. Chaplain Parker once again looked at the file, picked up the telephone and called the deceased inmate's brother.

—

The temperature climbed to the high nineties by mid-afternoon when Rob made the rounds in the non-air-conditioned B ward. The state of California did not have the money in the budget to get the air conditioners replaced or even repaired, so the heat made things even that more unbearable. Rob made his way from bed to bed to the end of the aisle, and took care of the patients' needs. He looked back at all the patients, but his eyes came to rest on an empty bed: Andy's bed. He just stood there and stared at it for a few minutes, numb. A patient's groan got his attention and he walked back down the aisle and stopped at inmate Robinson's bed. "Are you all right?" asked Rob. "I thought I heard you cry out?"

"It was that poor soul over there. Not me. You might check on him. Think he's been in a lot of pain the last few days."

"Okay, thanks," said Rob as he turned to walk toward the other patient's bed.

"Hey, hey… you," exclaimed Robinson.

"Rob, my name is Rob."

"Whatever," smirked Robinson. "I saw you. I was watchin' you… holdin' that old homo's hand when he died. Readin' him the Bible. What a bunch of hogwash! Just take a look around. There ain't no God! And, even if there was, He is one cold mother—"

"Look, that's enough! It meant something to Andy. He had peace. You don't have any peace. You're just a miserable old dope fiend dying of AIDS!"

"Ouch. You really know how to hurt somebody, boy. And, you call yourself a Christian?"

Rob turned and walked away, and stopped by Splinter's bed. "How ya doin', Splinter?"

"Robinson givin' you a hard time, Rob?"

"One bitter old man."

"Rob, I wonder if you could do me a favor?"

"Sure, what is it, Splinter?"

"I've asked other people, but they say they just can't do it."

"I'll try. I can't promise you, but you got my word... I'll try."

"I would like a Snickers candy bar. Can you get me one?"

"Uh, your chart says that you are diabetic. You can't have sugar, candy, stuff like that."

"Rob, my chart says that I have AIDS! What's a candy bar gonna hurt?"

"Ya got a point, kid. No promises. No promises."

"Hey, Rob. Don't pay any attention to old Robinson over there."

"Jacobs!" yelled Robinson. "Come back here, boy. I spilled my water. Give me another glass."

Rob returned to Robinson's bedside. He poured a glass of water for the inmate. "Here ya go," said Rob as he handed him the glass. Robinson reached out with a shaky right hand and grabbed the glass from Rob. It was then that Rob saw it for the first time. *How could I have missed it?* he thought. *It's the same tattoo.* It was the same green and red serpent on the right forearm of the robber who killed Rob's parents; the man he had vowed to kill. Rob was stunned and speechless. At first, he could not even think. It was as though his brain was frozen, but slowly it began to thaw, and grew to burn red with hatred for this dying inmate. *Finally,* he thought, *this man will pay for what he did... I'll make sure of it.*

143

CHAPTER 41

Bombshells

After the evening meal, Rob sat on the edge of his bunk and opened Jenny's latest letter. She wrote that Felix suffered a stroke, was in the hospital, but had recovered. Rob was concerned with that news, but then she dropped the bombshell, "I have filed for divorce." The words shocked Rob as though he had been shot by a stun gun. "Divorce?" he said out loud. "This can't be happening? Felix, my old friend, a stroke, and to top it all off the beast that killed my parents," he lamented. "Haven't I paid enough for what I've done, Lord? I don't think I can take all this—"

The hot summer sun bore down on the small Del Norte chapel like an open furnace. Chaplain Parker stood by the front door and fanned himself with the papers for his Sunday sermon, and waited for the inmates to arrive.

Rob came early, before anyone else arrived. Chaplain Parker was surprised to see him. "Rob, it's good to see you. You are looking well. How is everything going?"

"Not so good, sir. That's why I came early to talk to you. Jenny's divorcing me."

"What?" exclaimed Chaplain Parker. "I can't believe it. You two were so… together at the marriage seminar. I know she loves you. What happened?"

"I guess she couldn't handle it when she found out I tested positive and was transferred to Del Norte."

"I'm really sorry Rob. You know, I can only make phone calls in case of an emergency, but I consider this in that category."

"No, I think she's already made up her mind. I don't know what to do. I might as well kill myself!"

"Whoa, now that's the enemy talking. He wants to destroy you, take your soul. You've got to stay strong, Rob."

"I just don't know, Chaplain. Just when I was getting close, everything hits the fan. I'm getting those doubts again, those fears, and I feel an anger building up in me that I'm afraid I won't be able to control."

"You haven't gone through all of this for nothing. God has a purpose for your life. You may not know it at this moment, but God does. He has not left you. Don't forget about seminary."

"I don't know. I just don't know anymore."

"Rob, pray with me right now."

Something in Rob wanted him to resist praying with the chaplain, but he fought it off and surrendered. The two sat down in the front row of the small chapel. Chaplain Parker placed his hand on Rob's shoulder. A ray of sunlight streamed down on the two men like the beam of a spotlight on a soloist at a Broadway musical.

"Lord, I know you have a purpose in all of this," said the chaplain. "I trust in you, that you will reveal it to Rob in your time. You ordained marriage, Lord. I know you want to keep this marriage together, so I pray Lord that you put Rob and Jenny back together. Make them a family again. And Lord, I ask that you touch Rob and heal him from the top of his head to the bottom of his feet, Lord. Make him whole again. Restore his faith, and bring him that peace that surpasses all understanding. Amen."

Inmates were now streaming into the chapel like a river. Chaplain Parker made his way to the podium and welcomed the congregation. A small inmate choir gathered behind the chaplain and sang old hymns. Rob sat quietly and watched from the front row as tears streamed down his cheeks. *I don't think I can forgive Robinson,* he thought. *I need to confront him and if he denies it I will...*

CHAPTER 42

Tattoo of Death

Early Monday morning, Rob skipped breakfast and made his way to Doctor Chan's office where he found the doctor at work behind his desk.

"How are you feeling this morning, Rob?" asked Doctor Chan.

"I feel great. Looking forward to helping out on the ward today."

"Have a seat, Rob. I need to talk to you about something."

"My work? I'm not doing a good enough job?"

"Oh no, nothing like that. In fact, you are doing an excellent job. It's just that... your last blood test showed an increase in the HIV virus. This is a very fast progression that worries me."

"How can that be? I feel so good. Not tired or anything."

"I don't know. Perhaps your immune system is weakening? I don't know. What I do know, is that we need to do weekly testing. I am also going to increase your medication."

"Okay, Doc, whatever you say."

"Why don't you go on ahead and I will meet you up in B ward in about a half hour or so."

Rob walked toward B ward, but all he could think about was how he would kill Robinson. He became obsessed with the thought. It was all he could do to turn his thoughts and actions on to the other patients. He stopped at various beds to check on the wellbeing of the patients. The sound of coughing got his attention, so he went to investigate, and found out it was the youngest patient, Splinter.

"Splinter, you all right?"

"Rob. No, dude, just restin' my eyes," he said through a cough. "Did you bring me that Snickers today?"

"Uh, no. I couldn't find one. There's none to be found in this whole prison. Besides, what did I tell you about your diabetes?"

"Oh, don't be like that, Rob," hacked Splinter.

Rob moved quietly over to Robinson's bedside. Robinson's eyes were closed and he looked like he was asleep. Rob thought, *It would be easy just to smother him now with a pillow.* Rob looked around the room to see if anyone was watching. "Robinson," he whispered.

"What you creepin' up on me for? Scared me to death, Jacobs."

"I got to ask you something. Something about that tattoo."

"What about it?"

"When did you get it? How long ago?"

"I don't know, man. Why you ask? Got it in my twenties. Used to shoot dope right into that snake's mouth. Why you so interested in my tattoo?"

"Because the man that shot and killed my folks had *that* tattoo," said Rob as a matter-of-fact. "And, I vowed to kill him," he added with a tinge of anger.

Robinson's eyes grew big and he turned in his bed to look directly into Rob's face. "Your father? And Mother?" he asked. Robinson closed his eyes and slowly shook his head. "Ah man… That was your…? Look, I'm sorry, man. I was all doped up and didn't know what I was doin'. It's somethin' that's eaten at me my whole life. I'm so sorry, man."

"Well, saying you're sorry won't bring my parents back. Do you know how much that messed me up?"

"Go ahead, kill me Rob. You'd be doing me a favor."

But as much as Rob thought he wanted to kill him, all he felt in this moment was sadness.

"You know, I thought it would be easy to just, just, take your life like you took theirs… I've hated you for so many years… dreamed about killing you—"

"Forgive me, Jacobs. Could you ever forgive me? I know I deserve to die. That's probably why the Lord gave me this AIDS."

"I can't forgive you! I am going to kill you with my bare hands, but you won't know when. Maybe, you will be asleep or just resting your eyes. And, when you open your eyes, I will be there to put an end to your miserable life. It won't be today, but I guarantee you it will be soon."

Rob left the hospital ward and walked in a daze back to his cubicle and sat on his cot. A myriad of emotions flooded his brain. He picked up his Bible, opened it at random and began to read aloud, "Matthew 5, verse 38. 'You have heard that it was said, "An eye for an eye and a tooth for a tooth." But I tell you not to resist an evil person. But whosoever slaps you on your right cheek, turn the other to him also. If anyone wants to sue you and take your tunic, let him have your cloak also. And whosoever compels you to go one mile, go with him two. Give to him who asks you, and from him who wants to borrow from you do not turn away.' *But Lord, it's hard to turn the other cheek,* thought Rob. He continued to read aloud, 'You have heard that it was said, "You shall love your neighbor and hate your enemy." But I say to you, love your enemies, bless those who curse you, do good to those who hate you, and pray for those who spitefully use you and persecute you, that you may be sons of your father in heaven for He makes His sun rise on the evil and on the good, and sends rain on the just and on the unjust.' "Lord, how can I love my enemy?" said Rob. "How can I forgive him for taking the lives of my parents?"

Rob wrestled all night with God's word, with the ideas of vengeance and forgiveness. He knew what the Lord wanted from him, but it did not make his decision any easier. Early the next day, before breakfast, he went to B ward and stood next to Robinson's bed.

"I know my Lord would want me to forgive you, but I really don't want to," Rob sighed, "But… you *are* slowly dying and… I

148

have to forgive you. I don't really have a choice. I don't feel sorry for you, Robinson, but …I forgive you."

Immediately, it was as though a huge burden was lifted from Rob. This is what his Lord and Savior would have wanted.

"Thank you, son," said Robinson softly and closed his eyes.

Rob adjusted the same pillow he contemplated using to smother the inmate. "That any better?" he asked.

"Thanks, Jacobs. Lemme ask you somethin'… are you afraid to die?"

"What's that? Well, uh, no. I'm not afraid to die."

"I am. I'm afraid to die."

"What? A big bad dude like you? You never gave me the impression you were afraid of anything."

"Well, I *am* afraid… to die."

"I'm not," reasserted Rob.

"Why is that?"

"Because I know where I am going when I die," asserted Rob. "I'm going to heaven to be with my Lord. That's why I'm not afraid of death."

"I'd like to have that peace of mind."

"Do you mean it? All you got to do is be sorry for your sins; know that Jesus came to die in your place; everything that you ever said, did, or thought that displeased God… tell Him you're sorry."

"I'm sorry, Lord!"

"Now, just ask Him to forgive you, come into your heart, and tell Him that you will follow Him all the rest of your days, and thank Him."

"Forgive me, Lord, come into my heart. I will follow you all the rest of my days. Thank you, Lord, for everything."

"That's it, Mr. Robinson. You are now a child of God. He forgives you and has reserved a place for you in heaven."

"Thank you, son," said Robinson softly as tears trickled down his cheeks.

It amazed Rob how remarkable the Lord works. One minute he was ready to kill this man, and the next he was used to lead him to Christ. Rob continued his rounds checking on the patients until he was joined by Doctor Chan. Two nurses at the other end of the ward were changing IVs and bedding for several patients. A calmness fell across the quiet ward, a spiritual calm, as though it were a cathedral.

CHAPTER 43

Good News, Bad News

Doctor Chan stood by the window in his office as he read Rob's medical file. He occasionally looked out onto the vacant prison yard and reread the file several times. He shook his head in disbelief just as Rob entered. "Oh, Rob, just who I wanted to see," he chimed. "Have a seat," he added as he glanced toward the empty chair across from his desk.

"More bad news, Doc?"

"Rob, there's been a change in your blood work. The virus has… continued to increase. I'm sorry," he said as he hung his head.

"It's okay, Doc. I can handle it."

"The increase in medication hasn't done the trick. I—"

"Don't worry about it. I have a peace about it, Doc."

Doctor Chan just shook his head and stared at Rob's file, a look of sadness fell upon his face. "I'll meet you in B ward, Rob. Go on ahead."

Rob left the office and Doctor Chan continued to stare at the file as if in a state of disbelief.

—

Chaplain Parker finished reading a letter from Jenny and shook his head. "In my opinion this is an emergency," he said aloud as he picked up the phone and dialed the phone number in the letter.

"Hello?" answered Jenny.

"Hello, is this Jenny?" asked the chaplain.

"Yes, who is this?" Jenny replied.

"Jenny, this is Chaplain Parker, I was just reading your letter."

"Oh, hi Chaplain, I did not recognize your voice."

"Jenny, I am glad you asked me to pray for Rob, but I am saddened that you are filing for divorce. I know how much you love him."

"I do, Chaplain Parker. Everyone is telling me to divorce him. They're afraid he'll give the baby and me AIDS," she sighed.

"I can understand their fear. Much of it is the fear of the unknown. They need to get educated about HIV and AIDS. I'd be glad to talk to anyone in your family."

"Thanks, Chaplain. Just pray for Rob and me. I love him so much, and I've been thinking a lot about the right thing to do."

"You can count on my prayers."

"I appreciate that," she said. "You know Chaplain, that marriage seminar that you had taught me the importance of forgiveness and that God ordained our marriage. He doesn't like divorce, and in spite of what everyone is telling me, your call has confirmed in my mind that getting a divorce is not the right thing to do. I'm not going through with it."

CHAPTER 44

Contraband

Rob turned down the blanket on his bunk and prepared to go to bed. He placed his Bible on the small desk, and turned out the desk lamp. In the darkness he heard someone come into his space. "Who's there?" he asked sternly.

"Rob, Rob. It's me, Snoopy," he whispered.

"What do you want?"

"Chill, man. I just wanted to see if you changed your mind. You want anything? Cigarettes, drugs?"

"As a matter of fact, yeah, I do," stated Rob.

—

Rob made his way down the ward. He stopped at various bedsides along the way until he made it to Splinter's bed. "Hey, Splinter, wake up, dude."

Splinter woke from a sound sleep and tried to focus his eyes on Rob. "Is that you, Rob?" he asked drearily, rubbing his eyes.

"Dude, I scored," whispered Rob excitedly.

"What?" asked a bewildered Splinter.

"I scored! Look, I made good on my promise. Here," he said, holding out an object toward Splinter. "An extra-large Snickers!"

"You da man! You da man, Rob! This is awesome, dude. Awesome!"

"I'd better get back to work before Doc Chan fires me. Enjoy!"

CHAPTER 45

Visitor's Day

Visitor's Day at the prison was always hectic. The inmates that expected a visit from a loved one made sure they showered, shaved and primped for their prospective guest. Some would even iron their pants and shirts, and shine their shoes. They would try to hang around close to the outdoor visiting area or wait close to a speaker and listen for their name to be called over the public address system. On the other end of the spectrum, the guards were always on edge. They would be on the look out for escape attempts, fights, and the occasional act of smuggling drugs or other contraband into the prison. In all, emotions ran high on both sides for many different reasons.

It had been a few weeks since Chaplain Parker called Jenny and Rob had not heard from her since her letter that informed him she was seeking a divorce. So at first, Rob thought that he was mistaken when he heard his name broadcast over the loudspeaker. He listened carefully and heard it again. "Inmate Rob Jacobs. You have a visitor. Report to the Visitor's Center."

The outdoor Visitor's Center was already buzzing with visitors and inmates as they tried to find seating at picnic tables that were in the shade of the patio awnings.

Rob approached one of the guards on duty. "Excuse me, Officer Landry, I was just paged. I have a visitor?"

"Yes, over there," said Officer Landry, pointing to a picnic table in the visiting area.

Jenny stood up and waved at Rob, who walked briskly to Jenny, hugged her and kissed her gently on the cheek.

Officer Landry quickly approached them. "Jacobs, you know better than that. No touching!" he ordered. "If I see anything like that again, your visit is over," Landry advised as he turned back to his observation post.

"Rob, you look so good," sighed Jenny. "I expected you—"

"To look sick?" he said ending her sentence for her. "No, I feel good, and now that you're here—"

"Rob, I can't divorce you. I'm sorry that I told you that in my letter. I couldn't go through with it. I love you too much."

"Oh, Jenny, that's an answer to prayer! I don't know how I'd go on without you."

"Well, I have been praying too, and I know this is God's will."

"I want to hold you and kiss you so bad, I ache all over. This is a great surprise!"

"Rob, you only have a month left on your sentence! When you walk out the gate, Michael and I will be waiting for you with hugs and kisses ready!"

The two sat there transfixed on each other's faces, and stared into each other's eyes, not saying a word. Under the table, they played "footsie" with one another.

"Rob, the chaplain wrote to my mom about the unlikelihood of you giving everyone AIDS. But I am still concerned. Especially, about intimacy. I just don't know—"

"I understand, Jen. Please don't worry about that. Let's just take it one day at a time."

CHAPTER 46

Another Loss

Inmates had gathered in the dining hall for breakfast. The large room buzzed like a hive of bees. Rob went through the chow line and filled his tray. He spotted Snoopy and his posse and decided to sit with them.

"Hey, Rob," shouted Snoopy. "We haven't seen you in a while. Heard you lost another one last night in B ward?"

Snoopy's comment took Rob off guard. He hadn't learned of anyone passing. "Where did you hear that?" asked Rob in disbelief.

"You know, through the grapevine," replied Snoopy.

"What did you hear, exactly," challenged Rob.

"Just that some wanna be rock star kicked the bucket around three this morning."

Rob jumped up from the table, left his breakfast and hurried out of the dining hall.

"Say, brother, you gonna eat that?" yelled Snoopy as Rob was going out of the door.

Rob burst through the open doorway of Doctor Chan's office and blurted out, "Is it true? The kid in 14-B, the one they call Splinter... did he...?"

"Passed away due to complications from pneumonia about three this morning," stated the doctor as a matter of fact.

The wind went out of Rob's sails and his body went limp. He pulled up a chair and sat slouched across from Doctor Chan. "I didn't get a chance to say goodbye."

"Rob, you knew that it was inevitable."

Rob nodded, stood up, turned and started to walk away. "I'll be in the chapel, Doc."

"Meet me over in B ward when you're ready," said Doctor Chan.

Doctor Chan listened intently to the heart of one of the patients with his stethoscope as Rob approached and stood on the opposite side of the bed.

"When are you going to get some help, doc?" asked Rob. "We should have at least three doctors here, nurses, and... better equipment."

"I've been asking for help since the day I got here. Every year we get more and more prisoners with AIDS. I don't know how much longer I can go on."

"You can't go! What would happen to all these men?"

"Well, I'm way past my retirement age, but don't worry. I'm not going anywhere. But, if I wasn't a widower with no grandkids—"

"Hey, doc!" yelled inmate Robinson, interrupting the doctors comment. "What happened to that kid last night?"

"Died, about three," he replied as he walked toward Robinson's bed.

"Yeah, thought I was dreamin' when they took him outta here. Too bad, nice kid," said Robinson. "Always talkin' about his dog named Snickers or something," he quipped.

"How are you today?" asked Rob.

"What you see is what you get," he replied.

"Don't forget your meds. Here you go," stated the doctor as he handed Robinson a little paper cup that contained two or three pills.

CHAPTER 47

Miracles

Warden Reichert sat at his desk fumbling through a stack of papers when his secretary, Miss Rogers, entered and stood silently directly in front of him.

"Inmate Rob Jacobs, over in Del Norte, is due to be released in two and a half weeks. I want you to prepare the paperwork and schedule him for his final physical in the next day or so," ordered the warden.

"Yes, sir," she replied and turned to leave.

"Oh, and get me Chaplain Parker on the phone. Thanks," he added.

Several minutes later Miss Rogers returned and stuck her head in the warden's office. "Chaplain Parker, on line two."

The warden looked up, waved an acknowledgement, and picked up the phone. "Chaplain!" he chimed. "How are you?"

"Fine, Warden. Is there something I can do for you?"

"Just wanted to let you know that Rob Jacobs, your former clerk, is going to be released in a few weeks."

"I appreciate the heads up. You know, his wife changed her mind about the divorce," informed the chaplain. "A small miracle."

"That's great news. You know what a proponent of marriage I am," bragged the warden.

"Yes, while we're on the subject, how about another marriage seminar?" asked the chaplain with a wry smile.

—

Doctor Chan rummaged through his file cabinets and pulled out Rob's file. "Here, your latest blood test just came in. Let's see."

"Well, how is it, Doc?" asked Rob with anticipation.

The old doctor stared at the report, rubbed his chin and stated, "This can't be right."

"More bad news?" asked Rob.

"Just a minute," replied the doctor as he reread the report. When he finished reading it for the third time, he picked up the telephone and dialed the prison hospital.

"Hello, this is doctor Chan. I'm calling about lab results on inmate Rob Jacobs. There must be some mistake."

"Just a minute, doctor, let me find his file," stated the lab technician.

While they waited, Chaplain Parker entered the doctor's office and spotted Rob sitting across from the big desk. "Rob, I thought you'd be here or over in B ward. I wanted to make sure I said goodbye before you leave."

"Oh, hello, Chaplain," said Doctor Chan.

"Doctor Chan, so how's Rob doing over here?"

"Glad you asked," said the doctor.

"Yeah, we are checking on my final blood test. Hope I am not getting worse again."

"Just a minute," said the doctor raising a finger to his lips.

The lab technician read the results to the doctor over the phone and he repeated them out loud for everyone's benefit. "It shows a drop in the HIV level from 17,000 down to the normal range? That's... impossible!" exclaimed Chan. "It was on the increase."

"No, it's no mistake," stated the lab tech. "It is what it is... it's normal."

Doc Chan hung up the phone and stared across his desk at the chaplain and Rob with a stunned look on his face. "Impossible."

"What's going on?" asked the chaplain.

"Ya, doc, what's happening?" asked Rob impatiently.

"It's a… miracle. Your blood tests all came back normal. No HIV. Nothing!" exclaimed Doc Chan.

Rob leaped out of his chair and was immediately embraced by Chaplain Parker who administered a big bear hug.

"A miracle!" declared the chaplain. "God answered our prayers, Rob! First, your marriage, and now this! A miracle!"

"I'm healed?" asked a stunned Rob, who was immediately hugged by Doc Chan and Chaplain Parker in a three-way, jumping and dancing hug. "I am healed!"

Later that night, with mixed emotions, Rob made his rounds with Dr. Chan, and said goodbye to the patients, still reeling from the fact that he was no longer one of them.

CHAPTER 48

A New Start

The wind kicked up dust in the prison yard as the sun streamed through the storm clouds that had built up over the nearby mountain range. Earlier that morning, Rob woke up with a smile on his face for the first time since he was boy. This was the day he had waited for and dreamed about. Today was the day he was going to be released from prison. It was the day he would be going home. A new day, a new start.

Rob carried his few belongings and walked toward the exit gate. The pain in his leg seemed bearable. As he passed Sergeant Sharky, Officers Garcia and Smith, they all smiled and nodded at him. The gate opened in front of him and he walked through it to see Jenny, holding his son, and Felix standing by their side to greet him.

Jenny handed the child to Felix and ran to Rob and kissed him passionately. Rob then took his son and kissed his face. "This is what I have been fighting to stay alive for, my family." Rob reached out for Felix and hugged his neck, "And, my friends. I'm so sorry, Felix, for everything."

"Rob, I forgive you. I'm here for you, son," said Felix. "Welcome home."

"This is the best day of my life," stated Rob as he walked through the prison parking lot with his friend and family.

Several years later…

Chaplain Parker sat at his desk in the quiet prison chapel and looked through the day's mail. An envelope from R. Jacobs caught his eye and he hastily tore it open and pulled out the letter.

> *Dear Chaplain Parker,*
> *I pray that this letter finds you in the best of health. I apologize for not staying in contact with you. I cannot believe it has been three years since we last spoke. A lot has happened since then. My marriage is stronger than ever, my son, Michael, now has a little sister, Ruth, to play with and I graduated with honors from seminary. I have accepted a position to pastor a small church near Denver, Colorado.*
> *Thank you, for being my mentor, role model and inspiration. Like you always say, God is still in the miracle business. I witnessed first hand the miracle of my marriage being restore, the miracle of my healing, and the most wonderful miracle—God's forgiveness and gift of salvation.*
> *Love in Christ,*
> *Rob*
> *Just one of the Miracles at Del Norte*

Chaplain Parker sat and stared at the letter, almost as if in a trance. A lone tear trickled down his cheek and he quickly wiped it away, and then rubbed his watery eyes. It did his heart good to learn that one of his Christian inmates held true to God's promises. Rob was one of those former prisoners that did not return to prison within a year. The chaplain knew the sad fact that recidivism rate was horrible, even for Christian inmates, unless they had Christian support waiting for them after their release from prison. Eight out of ten inmates returned to prison, but Rob was an exception.

CHAPTER 49

Trinity

The small town of Trinity, Colorado awoke to a blanket of newly fallen snow from the season's first passing storm. A powdery snowfall glistened like sequins on a bride's gown from the early morning sun. On the top of a hill just south of the city, the tall steeple of the small white, wooden church seemed to glow like a beacon.

Pastor Rob Jacobs lit the fire in the potbelly stove that provided the heat for the little sanctuary. The smoky smell of the pine burning was one of the little things that the new pastor enjoyed. He had been up all night contemplating his first sermon, one that he had written before he was released from Del Norte. It was a message that meant so much to him personally, and he prayed it would be accepted by his congregation, and put into practice.

People began arriving before the stove could provide enough heat to warm up the little church. Rob wondered if his suit was free of wrinkles and if the tie his wife picked out was on straight. He hurried to the front door and began greeting his parishioners, giving each person a hearty handshake and wide, joyful smile.

A small six-member choir had arrived and entered through a rear door along with Miss Melody Hammerhill, the church organist. Melody was in her mid-fifties, considerably overweight and had played the church organ for over thirty years. She was perpetually surly and highly opinionated, which led to the reason she had never been married or even had a beau. It was Melody who voiced the loudest objection to hiring the new pastor. "What would people say if we hired an ex-con to be our pastor?" she bemoaned. "We're gonna lose all of our members." However, the deacons voted unanimously to hire the newly ordained former prisoner and slowly, but surely he won over the organist soon after his arrival.

The organ fired up and began playing the old familiar hymn, "Holy, Holy, Holy."

Rob turned toward the front of the church to see that it was almost full. His wife, Jenny, and their children, Michael and Ruth, were seated in the front row. One could not help but notice that Jenny was expecting their third child. She sat proudly with her Bible propped up on her stomach, waiting for the new pastor to take his place behind the pulpit.

The choir was in their position on stage and after the first hymn they began singing, "How Great Thou Art." Rob walked up to the front and stood to the side of the podium. He realized he was smiling too much when he noticed his cheeks were starting to ache, but he just could not help it and joined in singing loudly.

The old hymn was followed by another called, "Blessed Assurance," and then finally by the new pastor's request, "Amazing Grace." As the pastor, choir and congregation sang the last hymn, tears streamed down the pastor's face. This was the song that had such a special meaning to him. It was the one the prisoners sang every Sunday in chapel, and it was a reminder of God's amazing grace in his life.

Rob took his position behind the pulpit and looked out at the standing room only congregation. "Praise God," he said under his breath.

Jenny looked up at him and smiled. They had been through a lot in the last several years, but now they had given God control of their lives and serving Him was the desire of their hearts. She nodded at her husband in the affirmative, *Go ahead.*

He adjusted the microphone, cleared his throat, took a deep breath and looked out over the congregation who sat quietly with anticipation. The new pastor nervously began his first sermon,

"Welcome. Thank you all for coming, and thank you for making me and my family feel so at home. Most of you have probably heard of my background. Yes, I am an ex-convict," he stated as some of the people shifted in their seats. "But before that I grew up in southern California, a surfer boy, who accepted Christ as his Lord and Savior in high school. Both of my parents were murdered in a robbery when I was a kid, and I vowed that if I ever found the man responsible I would kill him. I am somebody who married his high school sweetheart. Somebody who joined the marines and shipped out to the Persian Gulf War, who saw some of his buddies die, and who nearly lost a leg. Somebody who became addicted to painkillers, which led to harder drugs and eventually to prison. Because of injecting heroin, I contracted HIV, and ironically that led me to the man who murdered my parents dying of AIDS in the same prison I was transferred to. Did I kill him like I promised? The hate was there. The opportunity was there." The congregation was so transfixed on the young pastor that you could have heard a feather land on the old oak floor of the tiny church. "No, I did not," he continued. "Instead, I forgave him and led him to the Lord. Believe me, it wasn't easy to give up the hurt, the anger, and the hate for what this man had done. However, I rededicated my life to the Lord in prison and I had no choice. He gave me the grace and the power to do it. You see, the Bible, in Matthew 6:14 and 15 tells us that if we forgive others of their trespasses, our heavenly father will also forgive us; but if we do not forgive others, neither will our Father forgive our trespasses. In other words, we must forgive to be forgiven. Mark 11:25 tells us not to hold anything against anyone, but to forgive them, so that your heavenly Father may forgive you of your sins. The Bible also tells us that in the same way we judge others, we will be judged, and with the same measure we use, it will be measured to us. When I forgave the prisoner with AIDS for what he had done to my parents, and to me, a tremendous weight was lifted off of my shoulders. It reaffirmed what the Lord had done for me on the cross: His forgiveness of my sins, past and future. It made it easier for me to forgive and lead that man to Christ. I believe it is because of my obedience to the Lord in this, that he graciously healed me of HIV and restored my marriage, my family, my life. If you consider yourself a born again believer, but there is someone you have not forgiven, then your salvation is not complete until you forgive that person. Remember, the Father won't forgive you of your sins until you forgive that person. If you do not know Jesus Christ as your personal Lord and Savior, you can begin that relationship right now. However, you need to understand that being a Christian means living for Christ. It is doing His will and not yours that matters. He said to deny yourself, take up your cross and follow Him. Following the Lord is not easy. He didn't promise you a rose garden, but even if he did, every rose has its thorns. The world will ridicule you, and Satan will try to put up roadblocks in your walk with Jesus. But praise God, greater is He who is in us, than he who is in the world. We are more than conquerors in Christ. 2nd Peter 1:3 says, 'His divine power has given us *everything* we need for *life* and *godliness* through our knowledge of him.' It is the power of Christ in us that enables us to forgive, to love, to serve. If you want this power in your life, and if you understand my message, repeat this prayer with me Dear Jesus, I know that I am a sinner. I humbly accept the sacrifice that you made on the cross for me. Please come into my heart, cleanse me of all my sins and give me eternal life. I repent from all my sins and put my life in your hands. Enable me to live my life in a way that pleases you. Thank you, Jesus. Amen."

Rob was stunned when the whole congregation rose to its feet and applauded. They were not necessarily praising the man, but showing approval of him and his message. He beamed from ear to ear, praising the Lord in his heart, as the choir sang Amazing Grace once again.

Later that evening, in the quiet solitude of his office, Rob reflected on the many miracles that occurred at Del Norte: the miracle of forgiveness; the miracle of healing; and the greatest according to Pastor Rob Jacobs, the miracle of a transformed life in Jesus Christ.

LaVergne, TN USA
21 December 2010
209694LV00001B/120/P